PUFFIN BOOKS

THE MORE
COMPLICATED
Crushes
OF LOTTIE
BROOKS

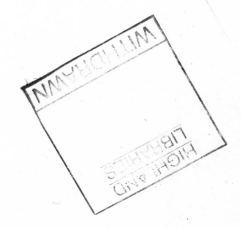

THE MEGA-COMPLICATED

Crushes

of

KATIE KIRBY

PUFFIN

PUFFIN BOOKS

UK | USA | Canada | Ireland | Australia
India | New Zealand | South Africa

Puffin Books is part of the Penguin Random House group of companies
whose addresses can be found at global.penguinrandomhouse.com.

www.penguin.co.uk   www.puffin.co.uk   www.ladybird.co.uk

First published 2022

001

Text and illustrations copyright © Katie Kirby, 2022

The moral right of the author/illustrator has been asserted

The brands mentioned in this book are trademarks belonging to third parties

Text design by Kim Musselle
Printed and bound in Great Britain by Clays Ltd, Elcograf S.p.A.

The authorized representative in the EEA is Penguin Random House Ireland,
Morrison Chambers, 32 Nassau Street, Dublin D02 YH68

A CIP catalogue record for this book is available from the British Library

ISBN: 978–0–241–56203–1

All correspondence to:
Puffin Books
Penguin Random House Children's
One Embassy Gardens, 8 Viaduct Gardens, London SW11 7BW

MIX
Paper from
responsible sources
FSC® C018179

Penguin Random House is committed to a
sustainable future for our business, our readers
and our planet. This book is made from Forest
Stewardship Council® certified paper.

To Felix and Seth,

who provide so much inspiration –

from the cheese-panini obsessions

to the fart jokes.

I love you guys more than

words can say x

TUESDAY 3 MAY

7.12 a.m.

OMG OMG OMG!!!!!

Today I have to see Wotsit Fingers and maybe even speak to him . . .

I know we chatted last night but that was just on WhatsApp. Today it will be **IN PERSON,** which is completely different because it involves ACTUALLY seeing him with ACTUAL eyes and ACTUALLY speaking to him with ACTUAL lips.

OMG!!

I REALLY don't want to go all BRINE-DOOPEY again and mess it up because it's been going so well . . . In case you've forgotten, we have an ACTUAL date.

OMG!!!!!!!!!

1

Anyway, I'd better stop obsessing over Daniel and get dressed and do my teeth or I'll be late for school. I will update you ASAP when I get home.

Wish me luck!

Note to self: you really must stop saying OMG so much.

4.14 p.m.

OK, I'm back.

So . . . as I was pretty late for school for reasons beyond my control, I didn't see Daniel at all until lunchtime.

There I was, standing in the lunch line with Jess, and he comes in with some mates.

Jess starts nudging me and going . . .

She clearly thought she was being really funny, when actually it was not very funny **AT ALL**. If I'd have been able to get a gag on her without drawing EVEN more attention to the situation, I would have, but instead I just gave her my best Death Stare.

I've been working on my Death Stare for about three and half years now. If you are interested in perfecting your own, here are my simple instructions:

How to perform the perfect Death Stare:

1. Open eyes really wide.

2. Tilt head slightly to the left.

3. Grit teeth while simultaneously pursing your lips.

4. Frown in a quizzical type of way that implies: **'WHAT ON EARTH DO YOU THINK YOU ARE DOING?!?!'**

The end result should look something like this

I mean, I'll admit it's not exactly the most attractive look, but it gets the job done and that's what it's all about.

Anyway . . . sorry. Back to the story . . .

Suddenly Daniel is right there in front of me, and he gives me a really strange look.

Erm, Lottie - what's wrong with your face?!

Oh, bum!!

That's when I remembered I was still doing my Death Stare – so I reorganized my facial features back into their usual positions.

Apart from the initial weirdness, you'll be really pleased to know that the convo went pretty well. I've written a transcript here as I know you must be **EXTRA MEGA INTERESTED** . . .

ME: Hey, Daniel!

DANIEL: Hey, Lottie.

ME: What are you having for lunch today?

DANIEL: I brought a cheese roll in. You?

ME: I'm getting a cheese panini.

DANIEL: Nice.

ME: Have you got crisps?

DANIEL: Yeh, Wotsits.

ME: Cool.

Five seconds of awkward silence

ME: Do you like Wotsits then?

DANIEL: Yeh.

ME: I thought you might . . . I just noticed that

	you eat them quite a lot . . . How often do you usually have them?
DANIEL:	Errr . . . not sure, maybe twice a week . . . Why? Are you monitoring my crisps consumption, Lottie?
ME:	NO! That would be weird . . .
DANIEL:	Yes, it would.
ME:	I just always find with Wotsits that the cheese powder can get a bit messy and sometimes it can get stuck under your fingernails, so you have to wash your hands extra super well afterwards . . . Do you find that too?
DANIEL:	Um . . . Maybe . . . I've not really noticed.
ME:	Hmmm.

Three more seconds of awkward silence

ME AND DANIEL AT THE SAME TIME: So . . .

Nervous laughter

DANIEL:	You still cool for next Saturday, yeh? Boho Gelato at 3?

ME: Yeh, great. See ya there!

I mean, it wasn't without fault. The cheese-powder part was maybe a *bit* intense, and I *may* have come across as a crisp-obsessed freak, BUT I did plant the seed about the potential cheese-powder-fingernail issue, so at least he's aware of the dangers now.

The most positive part was that all my words were **REAL ENGLISH WORDS** so I'm going to give myself an A+ for effort. Well done me.

THOUGHT OF THE DAY:
Must try and think of some conversation topics that don't revolve around crisps.

WEDNESDAY 4 MAY

NEWSFLASH!

Molly and Theo are officially 'boyfriend and girlfriend'.

The **WHOLE** of Year Seven is obsessed with the pair
of them. They are like proper celebs. Sort of like Justin
and Hailey Bieber . . . except they aren't married . . .
or millionaires . . . or American/Canadian . . . or even
actually famous, but apart from that they are REALLY
similar.

When they came into the canteen together at lunchtime, the entire place went silent and just gawped at them. You could hear a pin drop!

Amber seems to be pretending to be 'absolutely fine' with it but at the same time not being very fine at all. You can tell that she's super jealous of their rise to superstardom and would give anything to be in Molly's place . . . mostly by the way she keeps angrily stabbing her compass into the desk in nearly every lesson.

Things are OK between me and Molly now, but I haven't spoken to her much because she always seems to be with Theo or Amber. I'm really glad we sorted things out though.

Amber, on the other hand, STILL hasn't apologized for her behaviour at the party and I suspect she never will. The good news is that since she dumped Poppy as her BFF, Poppy has been hanging around with me and Jess, and we are becoming much better mates – we even have our own WhatsApp group that we use to discuss really important political stuff.

Oh, hang on – my phone just pinged. (How weird is that?)

Fries Before Guys WhatsApp group:

> **POPPY:** Who is your number-one celebrity crush?

> **ME:** Oooooooh tough one. But I'd have to go with Tom Holland because he's soooooooooooooooooooooooooooooooooooooooooooooooooooooooooooooooooooooooooooooooooooooooooooooooooooooooooooooooooooooooooooooooooooooooooooooooooooooooooooooooooooooooooooooooooooo gorgeous. And yes, I really do think he deserves that many 'o's.

POPPY: Yeh, I LOVE Tom Holland! Mine would be Leonardo DiCaprio.

JESS: WHAT?! Leonardo DiCaprio is SO old!

POPPY: I mean in his *Titanic* days OBVIOUSLY. That scene, when Rose lets go of him and he sinks down into the ocean makes me cry every time 😦

ME: Bit selfish if you ask me – she totally should have budged up a bit and let him on the door!

POPPY: I know – what a waste. He was SO good-looking.

ME: What about you, Jess?

JESS: Hmm, I think you guys should really stop objectifying these poor men 😕

POPPY: Say, what?!

JESS: My mum bought me a book on feminism and so far it's been an incredibly enlightening read. It's not really OK to make judgements about people based on the way they look.

ME: But I don't like Tom Holland just for his looks. I also like him for his ability to swing between skyscrapers with his web-shooter things. Does that make it OK?

JESS: I'm not sure. I'll have to see if there is a section in here on Spider-Man . . .

POPPY:

THURSDAY 5 MAY

Had an excellent dream that I was MJ in *Spider-Man* last
night . . .

Woke up feeling pretty disappointed that I was in fact
Lottie Brooks and instead of going off to help Tom
Holland save the world I was going into school to do a
maths test that I had forgotten to revise for . . . In case
you are interested, I ended up getting 15 out of 40 –
OOPS!

I'm pretty impressed with my Spider-Man drawing
though – maybe when I'm a grown-up I could get a job
as a Marvel cartoonist?!

SATURDAY 7 MAY

8.24 a.m.

In exactly one week, I will be going on a date with Daniel.

ONE TINY LITTLE WEEK! It feels ages away and also far too soon.

I wonder if he'll ask me to be his girlfriend?!?

I already feel sick with nerves . . . mostly because of the kissing dilemma. I mean, should we kiss on a first date? If so, should I kiss him? What if he kisses me? ARGH!!

I have no clue what will happen or what I actually want to happen.

In theory I like the thought of kissing him . . . but in reality it makes me feel all wobbly inside.

One of the main problems is that I have never kissed a boy before, so I have NO IDEA how to do it.

Have googled 'how to kiss' and there are 2.8 billion results – who's got time to read all that?! It would take approximately eight years or something and I'd be twenty years old by then. Still, at least it helps to know that a lot of us are in the same boat.

I read one or two articles and apparently I should 'relax', 'not overthink it' and 'let my lips guide the way'.

So that's all *really* helpful. NOT. I mean, what if your lips have no idea where they are going?!

Poppy messaged to see if me and Jess want to meet her in town. Asked Mum for twenty quid to take with me.

She said, 'What on earth do you need twenty quid for?'

I said, 'I dunno – food and stuff.'

She didn't seem to like my response very much. 'Money doesn't magically grow on trees, Lottie. I can't just give you twenty pounds every time you decide you want to *go into town* like it's some sort of sporting activity.'

'It is kind of a sporting activity,' I said. 'If you count riding up and down escalators in the shopping centre a sport – which I actually do.'

And in first place, about to make a pit stop in Zara, here comes Great Britain's Lottie Brooks!

Mum said, 'That's ridiculous, Lottie. Me and your dad work hard to earn our money, you know.'

So I said, 'You don't work! You just watch telly and go to the shops!' And she liked that response even less.

'For your information, I'm on maternity leave! I've a house to clean, meals to cook, clothes to iron –' which is untrue as she **NEVER** irons – 'and I'm barely getting four hours' sleep a night. It's hardly a holiday! Also, that's beside the point . . . What I'm trying to say is that if you want money to do things with your friends, then you will have to save up your pocket money or try to earn it.'

'I'm only twelve! I can't get a job – it would be child labour.'

'I'm not saying you should get a job, but I'm quite happy to give you extra pocket money if you do a few more chores around the house.'

'OK, fine. What can I do for twenty quid?'

'That's a lot of money, Lottie. But –' she looked around thoughtfully – 'I could give you £2.50 to tidy the sitting room, vacuum the floor and do the washing-up. How does that sound?'

Was she having a laugh?! What sort of world is she living in? That would take me like an hour or something and I don't have time for that – I'm incredibly busy worrying about kissing boys, for crying out loud! Plus £2.50 wouldn't even buy me a bubble tea.

So I said, 'Thanks for the offer, but no, thanks.'

Then I went to find Dad, who was hiding in the shed doing something manly (as usual).

'Mum said to ask you to give me twenty quid.'

'Really? What do you need it for?'

I did my best embarrassed face and said, 'Women's . . . *things*.'

Dad's entire head went bright red (he looked like a cricket ball – with a beard!) and then he quickly handed me a couple of ten-pound notes from his pocket.

Not just a pretty face, eh?

4.25 p.m.

Met Jess and Poppy in town. Molly was seeing Theo – yes, *again*! Don't know what Amber was doing. Probably still jabbing her compass into things for fun.

Mooched about, tried on a few clothes, and then I treated us all to sausage rolls from Greggs as I was feeling flush with my £20 windfall.

As we were leaving to get the bus home, guess who we saw . . . Molly and Theo!

They were standing just outside the shopping centre, sharing some chips.

'Quick! Hide!' said Poppy.

We all quickly hid behind the bus stop.

'Why are we hiding?' said Jess.

'Because . . . we . . . I don't actually know. Poppy, why are we hiding?'

'Just shhhhh – we are seeing what they are doing!' replied Poppy.

'OMG!!! I think they are going to kiss!' Jess squealed.

'NO WAY!' I said, peeking out round the corner.

'Oh no . . . False alarm . . . He's actually just wiping some sauce off her face.'

'That's sooooo romantic.' Poppy swooned.

'Is it?' said Jess. 'I thought buying someone roses was romantic. I didn't know it was as simple as wiping sauce off someone's face . . .'

I mean, I had to agree with Jess really, but it did feel weird seeing my BFF-since-I-was-five on a date with a boy. I still feel kind of sad that we aren't as close any more. I'll make sure I ask her about it at school on Monday.

THOUGHT OF THE DAY:
Imagine if I don't have my first kiss until I'm twenty years old! I really hope that doesn't happen!

SUNDAY 8 MAY

11.24 a.m.

It is slowly dawning on me that I need to inform my parents that I'm going out on a date with a boy next weekend. The thought of doing this fills me with **PURE DREAD**.

It's kind of like the time I had to say I wanted to wear a bra – BUT WORSE.

I'm not sure whose reaction I am most worried about. Dad will get all overprotective, Mum will get gushy, Toby will find the whole thing hilarious and make fun of me for ~~days weeks months~~ years, and Bella will just try and pull my hair out and vomit on me.

Decided to practise by telling the hammies, so I took them quietly to one side after lunch and broke the news to them. Spoiler alert – they weren't remotely interested! RUDE.

MONDAY 9 MAY

Cornered Molly at registration as I was desperate to find out about how things went on her date.

'How are things with Theo?' I asked.

She stared into the distance with a happy, wistful look on her face. 'Oh yeh, amazing. He's **SO** lovely. We went to McDonald's on Saturday and he bought me a McChicken Sandwich. I offered to pay – I *am* a feminist after all – but he insisted. It wasn't even a 99p one – it was a full-price proper one. How cute is that?'

'I mean . . . quite? I guess . . .'

'I want to remember it forever, so I kept this,' she said, pulling out a screwed-up bit of tissue from her pocket.

'What's that?!'

'It's his napkin.'

'Oh . . . um . . . lovely. Is that Big Mac sauce on it?'

'Yeh. He **LOVES** Big Macs,' she said dreamily.

Well, so do I but I don't want to keep screwed-up old napkins covered in them. However, I didn't want her to feel bad, so I just said, 'Wow. Cool. You could pass it on to your kids and grandkids like a family heirloom.'

'Yeh, I totally will,' she said while smiling and stroking it.

OK, I was being sarcastic, but it seemed totally lost on her today.

Then – get this – she kissed the napkin and put it back in her pocket.

What a strange girl.

Maybe this is what love does to you??

We'll have to see in a couple of weeks' time if I'm collecting Daniel's used napkins. Hope not – blurgh.

TUESDAY 10 MAY

At lunch, me, Jess and Poppy all ordered cheese paninis – FYI cheese paninis are **THE BEST THING EVER INVENTED** (apart from hair straighteners, Wi-Fi and Tom Holland obvs) and the only thing I ever buy in the canteen (apart from slushies, crisps, chocolate, cake, popcorn, waffles, etc., etc.).

So anyway, we were all sat at a table eating our cheese paninis and having a nice chat about how much we love cheese paninis (we always have the best conversations) . . .

. . . when Theo, Daniel, Amber and Molly walk in and start heading over to our table. I immediately felt my heart rate increase by like a million per cent.

'Mind if we sit with you guys?' asked Theo.

'Yes . . . I mean . . . no . . . I mean . . . plud ouu,' I mumbled.

PLUD OUU?!

ARGH! What did I even mean?! I was in danger of going all marshmallow-brained and BRINE-DOOPEY again.

'She means, that would be lovely!' Jess said, and laughed.

Honestly, what would I do without her?

'I thought we were going to sit on the sports field?' moaned Amber, but by that point Theo had already squeezed in next to Molly, and Daniel was taking a chair next to me.

'How are the cheese paninis today?' Daniel asked.

'**A-MAZING!** I'd definitely give today's a solid thirteen out of ten,' I said, thrilled to be using proper words again.

'That's just stupid. You can't get thirteen out of ten,' muttered Amber.

'You can with cheese paninis!' replied Daniel, and I felt really glad that he had my back.

Amber just sighed and shook her head like we were the stupidest bunch of people she'd ever come across.

I wondered why she was even talking to us, but then I caught sight of Molly and Theo at the end of the table – they were giggling together like they were in a world of their own.

'Those guys are just the cutest, aren't they?' said Poppy, following my gaze.

'They really are,' I agreed, nodding.

'Er, Lottie. Did you know that you've got cheese all down yourself?' interrupted Amber.

I looked down. 'No, I didn't,' I said, picking a stringy bit of cheese off my blazer. 'But thanks for that – I wouldn't have wanted to waste it!'

And then I popped it in my mouth and gave her a big grin.

She rolled her eyes and started gathering up her stuff. 'I don't want to sit in here. It's really sunny outside. Molly, are you coming?'

Molly didn't reply. She and Theo were too busy giggling over a private joke.

'MOLLY – are you coming or what?!'

'Errr . . . I'm OK here. Catch you later though, yeh?' she said before turning back to Theo.

With that, Amber picked up her bag and stormed off.

'Wow, what's got into her?' said Jess.

'She's clearly super jealous that she doesn't have a boyfriend,' said Poppy.

I almost felt sorry for her, but then I started thinking that if the situation was the other way round and she was the one with the boyfriend, she certainly wouldn't be worried about anyone else.

THOUGHT OF THE DAY:
I don't care what Poppy says.
I think having a bath in cheese
paninis would be awesome!

Nom nom nom!

THURSDAY 12 MAY

Only two days to go until the biggest event of my ENTIRE life! Apart from being born, I guess, as that was a pretty big event. The only other notable things that have happened are the births of my siblings, but they pale into insignificance against a date with **THE LOVE OF MY LIFE**. Sorry, I mean THE **POTENTIAL** LOVE OF MY LIFE. Sorry, I mean Daniel. (OMG CHILL, LOTTIE, CHILL!)

I finally told the fam about my date at dinner. I figured it was better to get it over and done with in one go rather than telling everyone individually and having to keep repeating myself.

I said, 'I've got a date on Saturday with Daniel, and we are going to get ice cream,' and then I just stared right down at my tacos, waiting for someone to break the silence.

Their reactions were **EXACTLY** as I had imagined.

Mum said . . .

Dad said . . .

Bella said . . .

And Toby stood up on his chair and started waving his arms and singing . . .

She wants to KISS him,
She wants to MAARRRY him!

I can't really decide which reaction I liked least, but Bella's was my favourite.

Still, I'm glad it's out in the open!

FRIDAY 13 MAY

7.55 a.m.

Woke up in a cold sweat. Had the worst nightmare.

It was about the date – Daniel didn't turn up!!

I was waiting in Boho Gelato for ages and then I noticed
that the whole of Year Seven were standing outside
laughing at me.

I realized it had all just been a massive joke and I started
to cry – I couldn't help it!

Then a film crew arrived, and the whole thing turned
out to be a prank for a new TV show called *The World's
Biggest Loser!* – so not only was I humiliated in front of all
my classmates but I was also going to be humiliated on
national television.

It was horrific and I ended up having to move house and then school and eventually continents!

Fast-forward to a year later, and I was living in a 3,000-floor skyscraper in Tokyo that had a slide from the top to the bottom. It was the longest slide in the world, and it took ten minutes to go down – it was **MEGA FUN**. Anyway, I was just beginning to make friends and get my life back on track when I started growing eyeballs on the ends of my fingers!

After science today, Daniel said, 'See ya tomorrow, Lottie!'

And I said, 'Just checking – we aren't going to be on the telly, are we?'

He looked at me strangely and said, 'Erm. No.'

But I guess he would say that, wouldn't he?!

Dear God, please let Daniel turn up on Saturday. On his own. And definitely not with a TV crew. And also – please, please never let me grow eyeballs on the ends of my fingers.

SATURDAY 14 MAY

8.25 a.m.

Woke up and did some yoga to try and keep calm and focused . . . Well, I did the warrior pose for thirty seconds and then got bored, but that still counts, right?

Dad's going to drive me into town and I'm meeting Daniel at 3 p.m. so that gives me just over six hours to get all nice and ready. Slightly cutting it fine, I know, but hopefully it will be OK.

1.23 p.m.

I forced myself to eat a Pot Noodle for lunch even though I wasn't hungry. Then I really enjoyed it so I had another one. Then Mum got a bit mad because she said eating two Pot Noodles for lunch is greedy and unhealthy. Especially when followed by two bags of Monster Munch and a KitKat Chunky. I guess she has a point. OOPS.

I do feel much better now though.

I put on a face pack, did my nails, and washed and properly blow-dried my hair (before putting it back up in a high pony, so it was kind of pointless – but at least it feels nice and clean).

I am going for the casual look because it's most 'me' – jeans, T-shirt, trainers, and I'm good to go.

Messaged the girls to show them the end result . . .

Fries Before Guys WhatsApp group:

ME: What dya think??

JESS: Um, you look exactly the same as normal?! 🥱

POPPY: Yeh, love what you've done with your hair 😅

ME: How rude are you?!? This is the result of hours of hard work!

JESS: Sorry, what I meant was that you ALWAYS look great 😊

POPPY: So, are you feeling nervous?

ME: Weirdly I'm feeling surprisingly calm. Just over an hour to go!

JESS: Good! Maybe you should try making a list of conversation topics, you know . . . so you don't start saying 'plud ouu' or 'brine doop' again.

POPPY: Or worse – talking about his Wotsity fingers!

ME: OOH, GOOD PLAN!

JESS: Always got ya back, babe 😉

POPPY: Good luck, Lottie!

ME: Thanks, girls. Mwah xx

2.15 p.m.

Good conversation topics for a date (that don't involve
Wotsits):

1. ~~Would you rather speak cat or dog?~~

2. ~~What's the longest you've ever gone
without taking a shower?~~

3. ~~What age would you like to get married?~~

4. ~~How long do you think you'd last in a
zombie apocalypse?~~

5. ~~Do you have a favourite item of
underwear?~~

6. ~~Have you ever eaten your own belly-button fluff?~~

7. ~~What do you think happens when you die?~~

8. ~~Have you ever weed in a swimming pool?~~

9. ~~Do you sometimes hear voices in your head?~~

10. ~~Do you think it's possible to grow eyeballs on the ends of your fingers?~~

Crossed them all out because I honestly can't think of **ANY** conversation topics that aren't disgusting, creepy or just plain weird!! Guess I'm just going to have to wing it.

2.28 p.m.

I was wrong. I'm not feeling at all calm any more. I'm feeling about as calm as a person who is about to parachute-jump out of an aeroplane or tightrope-walk across a river infested with hungry crocs. Or maybe a little less nervous than that, I suppose, because the risk of dying in my situation is probably significantly less? I could choke to death on a topping selection, perhaps?!? I think I'll just go for sauce to make it less risky.

This is all Jess's fault for making me write that **STUPID** list because now I'm even more aware of how bonkers my brain is!

6.35 p.m.

I'M BACK, BABY!

And now I'm officially someone who goes on dates . . . I'm dating . . . I'm a dater . . . I'm no longer a lonely jacket potater!

I know what you are thinking – shut up, Lottie, and tell us about the blimmin' date.

OK, OK . . . Jeez, keep your knickers on!

SO . . . due to my dad being one of those really annoying people who leaves about double the amount of time to get anywhere, we ended up being ridiculously early. Well, ten minutes early, which IMO is still ridiculous. I could have used those minutes watching TikToks or cutting my toenails, which are *slightly* on the long side at the minute . . .

Anyway, I didn't want to look too keen, so I decided to hide round the corner and watch the entrance of Boho Gelato, waiting for him to arrive.

Unfortunately, as I peered round the corner from my really excellent hiding place of *just standing there,* I had not banked on the fact that he would come up behind me.

So I . . . erm . . . screamed in his face. It probably wasn't a great first impression.

Soooooo – moving on . . . Daniel was wearing jeans, an Adidas T-shirt and box-fresh Air Force 1s (you'll have to imagine these cos I can't be bothered to draw clothes – I'm a busy girl, don't you know). I noticed he'd put gel in his hair and the front bit was sort of curled upward and looked dead cute. I couldn't believe I was on a proper date with such a gorgeous boy!

We walked into Boho Gelato and as usual I started feeling a bit stressed by all the choices . . . Ice cream or sorbet? How many scoops? Cone or cup? Chocolate, caramel or strawberry sauce? Sprinkles, marshmallows or nuts?! Do I try and keep the flavour combinations sensible, or do I go crazy and get bubblegum and mint choc chip? **NO**. That was a bad idea – I remembered it tasted like toothpaste. Yuck.

I looked over at Daniel and his brow was furrowed in concentration.

'I just never know whether I should try and match the flavours up like chocolate and fudge or lemon and raspberry, or whether I should just pick two completely random ones . . .'

I smiled. 'Let's go mad and get the strangest combinations we can.'

'Deal.'

It took us about ten minutes to decide, but in the end I went for jam doughnut and pistachio with chocolate sauce and he went for popcorn and orange sherbet with caramel sauce. We both opted for tubs, mainly as it's easier to eat.

We were lucky and managed to get a table outside, so we sat and ate our crazy combinations in the sun. The streets were buzzing with tourists, and it felt a bit like being in Paris. Not that I've ever been, but, what I mean is, I felt sort of cultured and sophisticated . . . Well, apart from the bit when I dribbled ice cream all over myself.

'Do you have brothers or sisters?' Daniel asked.

'One of each,' I said. 'Toby is seven and incredibly disgusting and Bella is four months old and also . . . erm . . . pretty disgusting.'

He laughed. 'Wow! I'm an only child. Must be pretty hectic in your house?'

'Yep! I mean, I tend to spend a lot of time in my room to escape them all and hang out with my hamsters.'

'Cool. I love hamsters . . . What are their names?'

'Professor Barnaby Squeakington and Fuzzball the Third.'

Daniel proceeded to laugh so hard some ice cream came out of his nose. Then he started to choke, and I looked round nervously, hoping that, if the worst came to the worst, someone else would be able to perform the Heimlich manoeuvre on him.

I passed him a napkin and luckily after he'd wiped his face he managed to stop spluttering.

'Sorry . . . it's just I love those names so much. Do you know what my pet rabbit is called?' he said.

I mean, what a stupid question – how could I possibly know that?!? I decided to be normal and polite though, so I said, 'No.'

'King Gilbert of Flopsalot.'

Now it was my turn to totally lose it.

'KING GILBERT OF FLOPSALOT?!?!'

'OK, OK, I know it's dumb . . . but I came up with it when I was seven . . .'

'Nah, I love it. It's a brilliant name.'

'Thank you – I'll have to introduce him to you sometime.'

'That would be great.'

Him and me. Me and him. We are basically the same, stupid-pet-naming people.

Just then my phone beeped.

Fries Before Guys WhatsApp group:

> **JESS:** This is your emergency Get Out message. Reply with Option A 'THIS BOY'S A TOTAL MORON!' to execute an intervention.

> **POPPY:** Or Option B 'THIS BOY'S AS DREAMY AS TOM HOLLAND' to err . . . not execute an intervention.

I smiled.

'What's up?' asked Daniel.

'Oh, nothing. It's just Jess wanting to borrow my erm . . . roller skates.'

I replied:

> Option B – no help needed. I REALLY like him!!! ❤

I looked at my watch. We'd been eating our ice creams and chatting for over an hour! I still had half an hour until I needed to meet Dad, so we walked slowly back through the Lanes.

The conversation had flowed so easily before but suddenly I felt stuck for anything to say.

'I . . . er . . . I . . . er . . .' I mumbled. I was terrified of where this was going. What on earth was going to come out of my mouth next? 'Do you think it's possible to grow eyeballs on the ends of your fingers?'

OH GOD!! Mouth – what were you thinking?!

Daniel laughed, but in a nice way. 'I don't reckon so, but it would be pretty cool if you could – you'd have crazy good eyesight!'

'I hadn't thought of it like that but, yeh, I guess you would.'

As we approached the shopping-centre car park, he turned to me and said, 'This has been fun.'

I grinned. 'Yeh, it really has.'

'Maybe we could do it again sometime?'

'YES, PLEASE! I mean . . . um . . . yeh, that'd be OK, I guess.'

Then we smiled awkwardly at each other for about thirty
seconds before saying goodbye. There was no kissing but if
I'm totally honest I think that was a relief as I'm not sure
I'm ready for that just yet.

On the way home, Dad asked if I'd had a nice time but
luckily he didn't grill me too much. I think he was well
aware that I'd be getting it left, right and centre from Mum
and Toby when we got home, and he was right because
they tried to corner me as soon as I got through the door.

I dashed right past them and went up to my room. I
wanted to write this all down before I forgot any of the
details of THE BEST DATE EVER!!!!!!!!!!!!!!!!!!*

*Can you actually call it THE BEST DATE EVER if it's technically
the only date you've ever been on?! Confusing.

Well, if I got off lightly with Dad earlier, I certainly didn't get away with it at dinner time. It was like the Spanish Inquisition. (I don't even know what that actually means, but it's something my dad says when we ask him what he's been doing in his 'man shed' for so long.)

'So, let's all talk about our respective days . . .' said Mum, who was trying to be subtle and failing badly. 'Hmm, who should go first? I know . . . LOTTIE!'

'I'm fine, thanks, actually, Mum. Maybe someone else wants to talk about their day . . .'

'No, they don't. No one else has even left the house. Now stop trying to avoid the subject. How was your date?'

'Fine.'

'Fine?! You can't just say *fine*. We need more details.'

'Yeh, we want to know if you did any disgustin' kissin' – BLURGH!' said Toby.

'OMG!!! Can't we just get rid of him or something?'

'TOBY! That's enough of that,' warned Dad.

'So . . . come on, Lottie. Don't leave us hanging,' said
Mum.

'OK . . . It was . . . nice.'

Mum sighed.

'Oh, stop giving her such a hard time, Laura,' said Dad.

I shot him a thank-you smile.

'One more question and then I'll be quiet, I promise . . .
Are you going to see him again?'

'Yes, we go to the same school, so that's inevitable.'

'Don't be facetious, Lottie. You know what I mean!'

'OK, yes, Mother. Well, I hope so anyway.'

Blimey, I feel like I've been grilled more than a cheese panini!

OK, I have a confession. Before we left Boho Gelato, I grabbed the napkin that Daniel wiped his face on and stuffed it in my pocket.

I am now in bed cuddling it.

The regurgitated ice cream has dried into a crust but there is no escaping the fact it came out of Daniel's nose.

THOUGHT OF THE DAY:

Am I really disgusting?!

Actually, don't answer that.

SUNDAY 15 MAY

OMG, I'm on cloud nine this morning! (Whatever that means?!)

I feel like a magical unicorn running through beautiful fields full of pastel-coloured flowers.

If this is love, then I'm sold because it feels awesome!

EWWW, sorry about that freaky picture. I look like a messed-up version of Mr Tumnus. Not good. OK, I'm scribbling it all out. YUCK.

WHEEEEEEEEEEEEEEEEE! I got a message from Daniel . . .

DANIEL: How are you today, Lottie? D x

ME: I'm good! I feel like a unicorn!

DANIEL: What?!

ME: Oh, sorry. I mean, yeh, I'm fine.

DANIEL: You are seriously weird, Lottie Brooks!

ME: In a good way or a bad way?

DANIEL: In a good way!

ME: A bit like an anteater? They are weird in a good way.

DANIEL: Erm yes. Just like an anteater 🥲

ME: I'm really not sure I'd like to eat ants though. 🐜 🍴 🤢

DANIEL: That's a shame cos I make a really good ant pasta bake!

ME: Really?!

DANIEL: NO!!

ME: 😴

DANIEL: Gotta dash. See ya at school tomo! X

ME: Yep see ya! Xx

WOOHOO! I'M JUST SO HAPPY – NOTHING COULD RUIN MY MOOD TODAY!!!!!!!!!

Tell a lie – that's my lovely morning in Unicorn Land **TOTALLY RUINED**!

Toby just burst into my room, ran right up to me, pressed his horrible little bottom into my arm and did a massive fart.

Back to earth with a big bump.

MONDAY 16 MAY

Woke up this morning feeling **GREAT**! I usually hate
Mondays because getting up early and going to school is
URGH URGH but today I didn't mind at all because I was
so excited to see Daniel.

The feeling didn't last long though because my first lesson
was history and I got into **HUGE** trouble. Mr Simmonds
was talking to us about the plague, and it was so depressing
and grim that I started doodling in my exercise book.

Next thing I knew, Mr Simmonds suddenly goes: 'Miss
Brooks, I have just informed the class that approximately
fifty per cent of the population of Europe was wiped out
by the Black Death. Could you please explain why that fact
is causing you to sit there grinning like the Cheshire cat?'

'Oh, um . . . that's actually terrible, sir . . . I wasn't actually
grinning. I was just . . . taking some notes.'

'Well, I'm so pleased to hear that I was wrong. Let's take a
look at your notes, shall we?'

'Umm . . . well, I've not . . . done that much . . . yet.'

He picks up my exercise book, gives it a quick glance and does a big sigh. 'Well, this is incredibly disappointing, Miss Brooks. I see that instead of listening carefully as I talk about one of the greatest catastrophes in human history, you are doodling love hearts with **L 4 D** written in them.'

All around me I could hear my classmates trying to suppress their giggles.

'And what is this?' he continued, holding up my book for everyone to see. 'Is that your head on some sort of weird anteater-type creature?'

MEGA CRINGE!

The class erupted into laughter, and I wanted to die. As if the humiliation wasn't enough, he also gave me a bad-behaviour mark!

The only positive was that Daniel isn't in my history class so at least I spared him the embarrassment of going through that too.

The annoying thing was that I hardly saw him though. We smiled at each other across the corridor between lessons, but I couldn't see him at all during break or lunch.

Bit sad about it TBH.

TUESDAY 17 MAY

I bumped into Daniel after maths. We said hi to each other and then his mate Ben jabbed him in the ribs, and they laughed and walked off.

What does this mean?! Is he embarrassed by me?!

It's been three days since our date. I've barely said two words to him in school and he still hasn't messaged to arrange our next one. Surely he should have by now?

I don't know what I was expecting really – just that things would feel a bit different, I guess . . .

WEDNESDAY 18 MAY

4.15 p.m.

At registration, Molly scooched over to sit next to me.
'SOOOOO . . . how did the date go?'

I couldn't help but grin. 'Really great. We had ice cream,
chatted about our pets, and then he said we should go
out again soon.'

'**EEEK!** Lottie, that's so exciting!'

'I know!'

'So when are you seeing him next?'

'Well, that's the thing. I'm not sure . . . We've not
arranged anything else yet . . .'

'He's probably just been busy . . .'

'Yeh, maybe . . . I was getting a bit worried that he'd gone off me . . .'

'No way! Theo says he **REALLY** likes you. I'm sure he'll message you today or tomorrow.'

But I didn't see him for the rest of the day and now I'm back home and I've still heard nothing. I really hope Molly is right.

Oh, hang on. Someone just knocked on my door. BRB.

(4.56 p.m.)

I could absolutely kill Toby!!!

He came in my room to fart on me again and this time it was right in my face!

'URGH! You're disgusting – my room is not some sort of farting area!!!' I shouted.

'**HA HA** – hope you enjoyed my tasty air biscuit!'

'I one hundred per cent did not enjoy your horrible *air biscuit* – it smells like rotting cabbages!'

'Don't lie – you **LUUUURVE** my tasty air biscuits!'

'OMG, I'm telling Mum!' I said, shoving him back out of my room.

'MUM, TOBY JUST FARTED RIGHT IN MY FACE!'

'MUM, LOTTIE JUST HIT ME!'

'I DIDN'T HIT HIM!'

'OWW! MUM MY ARM FEELS ALL BROKEN!'

Toby throws himself on the floor and starts writhing around in mock pain like a premiership footballer just as Mum appears. I have to hand it to him – he's an A+ faker.

'Lottie Brooks! Why on earth do you think it's OK to hit your seven-year-old brother?'

'I barely even touched him!' I said, rolling my eyes. (FYI,

this was a massive error, as rolling my eyes NEVER goes down well with my mum!)

'Don't roll your eyes at me, young lady! Right, give me your phone now. You are on a screen ban for the rest of the day.'

'But you can't do that! I'm waiting for a very important –'

'Phone. Now!'

I reluctantly handed her my phone while Toby mouthed **'HA HA'** behind Mum's back.

So now I've lost my phone and I'll have no idea if Daniel has messaged me or not. Great.

THURSDAY 19 MAY

Mum just gave me my phone back this morning and
I turned it on excitedly hoping to see a message from
Daniel and – NOTHING.

Not sure what is going on. Is this what it's like to be in
a relationship? Because it started out fun and now it
doesn't seem very fun AT ALL.

I said to Poppy at lunch, 'I've hardly spoken to Daniel this week. Do you think he's avoiding me?'

'Nah, that's totally normal,' she replied. 'I mean, I've been going out with a guy called Sid for four weeks and I'm not even sure who he is . . .'

'What?! That makes zero sense. How are you going out with someone if you don't even know who they are?'

'Well, his mate Jamie asked me out for him, and I just said yes because I wasn't going out with anyone else, so I figured . . . why not?'

'That's mad! And why didn't you tell us?' said Jess.

'Well, TBH I'd kind of forgotten.'

'You'd forgotten?!'

'Yeh . . . Maybe I should try and find out who he is . . .'

'I really think you should,' I agreed.

I kept looking for Daniel for the rest of the day, but we didn't have any classes together and I only saw him from a distance. I looked for him after school too and then remembered he had football practice.

Now I'm just sitting in my room looking at my phone, willing it to ping.

4.20 p.m.

Silly me. He's still at football practice. It finishes at 4.30 so he'll probably message me then.

4.31 p.m.

He probably wants to get changed before messaging me, I suppose.

4.40 p.m.

He probably wants to get home first too . . .

5.04 p.m.

Maybe he wants to eat dinner first?

5.30 p.m.

Maybe he needed a shower?

5.45 p.m.

Maybe he's taking a nice long bubble bath?

6.06 p.m.

Well, I've been rather patient, Daniel, but now I feel like you are just being incredibly rude!!!!

> **THOUGHT OF THE DAY:**
> So, it seems that even when you go out with someone and have a nice date, that doesn't mean very much in school hours where you just pretty much ignore each other?! I guess I'm doing better than Poppy though. At least I know who I'm meant to be going out with.

FRIDAY 20 MAY

7.45 a.m.

Today is already going badly.

Woke up, went downstairs, and Mum goes: 'Remember you have the dentist this morning, Lottie. I'll drop you off at school after your appointment.'

Urgh, can't bear the dentist. We've had the same one, Mr Biggins, since forever, and he's a real killjoy. Always lecturing you for eating sweets, drinking fizzy drinks and not cleaning your teeth properly. Like – where is the fun in life? Yawn.

5.10 p.m.

Dentist was bad. Very bad.

Not only did I get a lecture about plaque build-up and making sure I brush my teeth for a full two minutes twice a day (who has time for that?!) but apparently my teeth are all wonky at the front too, from when I used to suck my thumb, so he suggested that I needed braces.

I said in no uncertain terms, **'ABSOLUTELY NOT!'**

'Oh, Lottie, stop being so dramatic!' said Mum. 'If we don't sort them out now, you'll end up looking like a donkey, and you don't want that, do you?'

Charming!

I replied, 'Well, FYI maybe I'd actually like to look like a donkey, thank you very much. Have you ever considered that?'

She didn't really have a comeback to that, so I thought maybe I'd won the argument until Mr Biggins said he was going to take impressions of my teeth and filled my mouth with some disgusting putty stuff that made me gag. Then he said they'd be in touch to make an appointment to get the braces fitted.

Had they not been listening to me AT ALL?!

I was outraged, I tell you. Especially because at the end, despite the fact I'm in high school, he offered me a sticker. Being such a nice, polite person is my downfall. I took it and put it on my school jumper without really thinking.

CRINGE

I WAS BRAVE!

Then – and this is the worst bit – I completely forgot about said sticker, and when I arrived late at school and joined the class midway through geography, Amber started clapping and said, 'Oh, well done for being such a big brave girl at the dentist, Lottie Potty!'

I wanted to die. I ripped the sticker off, rolled it into a ball and threw it at her.

'Sir! OWWWWWW – she hit me in the eye! She could have blinded me, sir. OWWWWW!'

Mr Bishop went: 'Girls, please! I am trying to teach a very important lesson on limestone formations and all I can hear is you two screeching. I'm afraid I'm going to have to give you both bad-behaviour marks and if I have to warn you again I'll send you to Mrs McCluskey's office!'

ARGH. That's two bad-behaviour marks this week! If I get five in one term, it means the school will phone my parents.

PS Number of messages from Daniel is still a big fat **ZERO**! Although he did wave at me after school, so I think that's a good sign.

SATURDAY 21 MAY

9.09 a.m.

Woke up feeling optimistic. Today's the day I'll hear from Daniel. I can feel it in my kneecaps.

NB I'm really not sure why I called one of my kneecaps Dave, but I quite like it!

12.12 p.m.

Just spent forty-eight minutes staring at my phone, willing it to ping. It was very boring/frustrating, and it didn't even work.

Mum came in and said, 'A watched pot never boils . . .' which apparently means that if you are looking at something and waiting for it to happen, it won't happen, but if you aren't looking at it, it probably will happen.

I'm now trying to think of somewhere to put my phone where it won't be easy for me to get it. Hmmmm.

(12.45 p.m.)

I'm a genius. Have buried my phone in a flowerbed in the garden using my old pink plastic Barbie spade that I found in the shed.

I certainly can't just have a quick look at it now! I'm going to leave it there for at least three hours and do something totally different instead.

(12.49 p.m.)

Can't really think of much else to do. My phone is basically my only hobby.

Thank God, Jess has come over. She knocked on the
door panting like she'd just run a marathon and said,
'I've sent you three messages and you didn't reply so
I thought maybe something bad had happened as you
ALWAYS have your phone on you.'

'Chill out, Jess,' I replied. 'I'm clearly still alive! I've just
buried my phone in the garden, that's all.'

'Oh . . . that's weird. Why?!'

'Have you never heard of the age-old saying "a watched
phone never gets any messages from boys you like"?' I
told her, sighing.

'Um. No. Lottie . . . are you feeling OK today?'

'Yes, I'm perfectly fine. But I'm glad you are here as I was
just getting very bored without my phone.'

'OK, well, what would you like to do?'

'I'd like you to amuse me, please.'

'What, like . . . do you mean tell you a joke or
something?'

'Err . . . OK, yeh, tell me your best joke.'

And this is the best she had (God help her) . . .

'Now what shall we do?' I asked.

'Well . . . would you like to look at TikToks on my phone?'
she said.

'Yeh. Good idea.'

1.45 p.m.

The phone has been buried alive for one hour now. Do phones need to breathe air? I hope it's OK.

2.45 p.m.

That's two hours. I'm sure it's filling up nicely with WhatsApps by now.

3.15 p.m.

Two and a half hours. It must be literally bursting with messages! Daniel's probably sent me at least two, or four, or maybe ten!

I said to Jess, 'I bet Daniel's sitting at home panicking about how I've not replied to him yet.'

'Yeh, he's probably a nervous wreck.'

'Well, he'll just have to get used to the fact that I've got better things to do with my time than stare at my phone, waiting for him to message.'

'Yeh, like burying your phone in the garden and staring at my phone instead.'

'Exactly.'

3.40 p.m.

I can't take it any more! We are off to the garden armed with my pink plastic Barbie spade to dig up that bad boy!

4.42 p.m.

We've been digging for an hour, and we can't find the blimmin' phone! I'm sure I buried it next to the purply plant thing.

4.52 p.m.

The problem is that there are more purply plant things in the garden than I thought.

4.59 p.m.

Finally found the phone. Jess called it and we traced a

faint ringing sound to the right of a pinky plant thing.
My bad – I thought it was more purply. Now to read my
messages!

ABSOLUTE WASTE OF A DAY.

Number of messages from Daniel: **ZERO.**

I can't believe it. He doesn't message me when I'm
looking at my phone or when it's buried in the garden
either. GO FIGURE?!?

Mum's also pretty mad about the state of the garden.

She's totally failing to see that if she'd not filled the garden with an abundance of the same-looking pinky/purply plant things, then it would have been much easier for me to locate my phone.

So basically it's her fault.

Oh, and I think Daniel should probably take some responsibility for this too because if he had just messaged me when I'd wanted him to, then I wouldn't have had to totally destroy the garden, would I?

7.47 p.m.

How mad is this – the police have just been over.

Apparently they had been alerted by 'a member of the public' about suspicious goings-on in our garden and they were duty-bound to come and check it out. Basically they thought I was trying to bury a body in the flowerbed!!

Mum made me explain to them exactly what I'd been up to, which was mortifying . . .

By the time they left, they seemed satisfied that I wasn't a murderer.

I think.

SUNDAY 22 MAY

3.04 p.m.

Things that are rubbish in my life:

1. Two bad-behaviour marks in one week.

2. Having the most disgusting little brother in the entire world.

3. Have to get braces when am on brink of having my first kiss.

4. Or not, because boy I like has gone AWOL and may not even want to kiss me anyway?!?

5. TBH I'm not sure I even want to kiss him either, as kissing looks gross/scary!

6. Only twelve years old but already a police murder suspect.

7. Mum is making cottage pie for dinner.
VOM.

3.22 p.m.

I want to cry. I have no idea what is going on with Daniel. Last week we had an amazing date and this week we've said about three words to each other.

Man, relationships are **SO** complicated!

3.33 p.m.

Sent a message to Jess:

> **ME:** Still NOTHING!

> **JESS:** I've had an idea. This might seem crazy but why don't YOU message HIM?

> **ME:** You want ME to message HIM?!

JESS: Yeh, why not? This is 2022 now, Lottie. You don't have to sit about waiting for boys to do all the asking. I mean, are you a feminist or what?

ME: Um, yes, I absolutely think I am a feminist!

JESS: Lottie, do you know what a feminist actually is?

ME: Of course! It's someone who opens their own doors and wears trousers.

JESS: No, Lottie!

ME: Well, what is it then?

Four-minute gap

JESS: Feminism is a range of social movements and ideologies that aim to define and establish the political, economic, personal and social equality of the sexes.

ME: You just read that directly out of your feminism book!

JESS: I SO DID NOT!

ME: What does it mean then, huh?

JESS: Look, you can't expect me to be an expert on the subject – I'm only on page 36 – but basically it means you should text Daniel.

ME: Jeez, you are so bossy!!

JESS: And proud of it ☺

ME: Do you seriously think it's a good idea though?

JESS: Well, it's better than getting interrogated by police on suspicion of murder ☺

She may have a point.

Inspired by Jess, I spent the afternoon researching feminism and I learnt all about this thing called the gender pay gap and now I'm fuming! Did you know that women earn significantly less than men for doing the same jobs?!

I am part of a new generation that can help change this appalling inequality!

We will not stand for it any longer and change starts **RIGHT HERE, RIGHT NOW** . . . with me texting Daniel.

(TBH I'm not entirely sure how me texting Daniel will help close the gender pay gap but it's a start . . . and, as Dad says, 'Rome wasn't built in a day!')

I spent the last forty-five minutes composing a text that expresses my new feminist viewpoints and also asks Daniel out on a date, and I've just sent this:

ME: Hi Daniel, did you know that on average women earn 7.9% less than men? Shocking, isn't it? Wanna hang out again soon? Lottie x

6.12 p.m.

OMG, he's replied already!!!! And guess what! Jess was right – he *was* hoping that I would message him! Thinking about it, it has been him making all the effort so far, so I guess it was my turn.

DANIEL: Hi Lottie, I didn't know that but I'm glad I do now. It is shocking! I was hoping you'd ask me that though. What are you up to over half-term? X

ME: Well, I have a few plans . . . but I'm free Tues or Weds?

DANIEL: Weds is good for me! X

Me: Great 😊 x

OMG, how easy was that?!

(FYI I don't actually have any plans over half-term, tee-hee!)

THOUGHT OF THE DAY:
Always remember it is totally acceptable to message a boy and ask them out yourself, and it is a much, MUCH better option than burying your phone in the garden.

MONDAY 23 MAY

Poppy is devastated. She finally found out who her 'boyfriend' Sid is, and she was really pleased as he looked lovely. Unfortunately, it turned out that he'd forgotten he was meant to be going out with her too and was now going out with Erin in Seven Red.

We tried to console her but apparently it was hard for me and Poppy to understand as neither of us has ever dated someone for an **ENTIRE MONTH**!

I didn't really have the heart to point out that technically they weren't 'dating' because neither of them had a clue who the other one was until yesterday.

She did start feeling much better after the lollipop though, so maybe Chupa Chups do help cure a broken heart? It was watermelon, which IMO is the best flavour!

TUESDAY 24 MAY

Told Molly that I was seeing Daniel over half-term, and she said that she was seeing Theo too and so we both looked at each other and screamed.

Unfortunately, this was in history again, so I got another bad-behaviour mark – EEK!

After class had finished and we were on our way to the next lesson, Molly said, 'So, what should we do for our double date, do you think?'

'I dunno. Let's chat to the boys about it tomorrow?'

'What's this? What are you guys doing?' asked Amber, looking a bit annoyed.

'Oh, me and Lottie are going to go out with Theo and Daniel over half-term, that's all,' replied Molly casually.

'Really? I was kind of hoping we could hang out . . .' (She said this to Molly, not me, obvs.) 'My parents are working, so I'm going to be on my own a lot of the time.'

'I'll hang out with you too, silly. It's just one day!'

'Yeh, I mean, we'd invite you along as well . . . if you had a boyfriend . . .' I said.

She shot me proper evils and I felt a little bit bad. I didn't want to be unkind, but sometimes she acts like she owns Molly and no one else is allowed to be her friend.

WEDNESDAY 25 MAY

You would not believe the latest news! Or maybe you would . . .

Amber is going out with Laurence from Seven Yellow.

Everyone is in complete shock. Largely because Laurence and Amber are like chalk and cheese – he is an uber-geek and president of the Dungeons and Dragons club, and she is uber-shallow and president of the **I ONLY CARE ABOUT MYSELF** club.

I know they say that opposites attract but I don't for one second believe that's the reason they are together.

My theory (supported by Jess and Poppy) is that she needed to get together with someone super quickly because she is *not-so-secretly seething* about me and Molly having boyfriends when she doesn't. (Not that Daniel is officially my boyfriend – yet.)

I mean, it's not very fair on poor Laurence, but TBH he looks delighted. I guess, for him, going out with the most popular girl in Year Seven is a once-in-a-lifetime opportunity, whatever the reason behind it.

FRIDAY 27 MAY

Walked home with Jess, Molly, Amber, Poppy, Daniel and
Theo and I felt really mature hanging out with the boys
too, sort of like proper adults.

We stopped off at the fish and chip shop on our way. A
lot of the kids from Kingswood High go there after school
on Fridays, which is funny because it's called **FRYDAYS** –
geddit? Personally, I love a good pun. If I owned a chippy
I'd call it Friendchips and I'd give all my mates a fifty per
cent discount because I'm nice like that.

Mostly it's the older kids who hang out there, but lately
more of the Year Sevens have started going too. The girls
all stand about twiddling their hair in the hope that the
boys will buy them some chips. You wouldn't catch me
doing hair twiddling though, as it's not very feminist
behaviour – see, I'm quickly becoming an expert!

You can tell how much someone likes someone else by
the type of chip purchase they make. We made up an
unofficial scale called the **CHIPOMETER OF LOVE**.

Basically, if you're single you buy your own chips, but if you're going out with someone OR want to be going out with someone, then this is how it works . . .

Interested in someone: chips.

Really like someone: chips AND curry sauce.

Practically in love: cheesy chips!

Soulmates: chips and a battered sausage on the side.

The chipometer of L♥ve

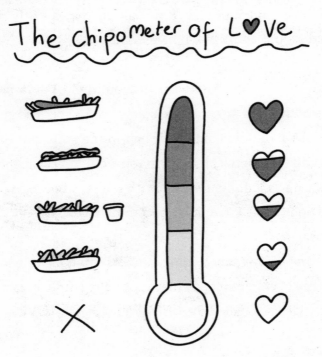

'You want some chips, Lottie?' Daniel asked.

Inside, I'm like *OMG OMG!!!!!! He wants to buy me chips so he deffo still likes me.* But then I remembered about being a feminist.

So I said, 'I do. But I'm a modern woman, so I'll buy them myself!'

He looked a bit confused, but Jess gave me a high-five. I think that means I'm getting it right now.

It was such a sunny afternoon that once we'd all collected our orders (Theo bought Molly chips and curry sauce – WOW!) we went to sit on the green opposite the chippy to eat them.

We started talking about what to do on our double date next week.

'How about bowling?' suggested Theo.

'I'm in!' said Daniel.

'Yes, that sounds fun,' said Molly.

I didn't think it sounded fun at all because I'm terrible at bowling unless I use the gutter-blocker things that generally become socially unacceptable after the age of six.

I didn't want to be the difficult boring one though, so I just said, 'Bowling is cool with me!'

We're going next Wednesday at 3 p.m., followed by dinner afterwards. We considered going to McDonald's, but then decided to be dead classy and book Pizza Hut instead.

I'm going to a proper restaurant with a boy I like – wahooooo!

SATURDAY 28 MAY

Woke up and watched some YouTube videos on bowling techniques.

I keep having visions of the last time I went when I forgot to let go of the ball and bowled myself down the lane too. The staff thought I'd done it on purpose and gave me a warning. They wouldn't believe that it was because I'm just **REALLY** bad at bowling.

Why does this sort of thing never happen to anyone else?!

SUNDAY 29 MAY

Bella has learnt to roll. She rolls around the floor until she gets stuck up against something like the wall or the couch and then she gets super mad and screams until someone moves her, then she does it all over again. And again. And again. It's like a **SUPER-FUN** game. Not.

The thing that's most annoying is the sound she makes: it's like a high-pitched shriek and it sounds like **'GAHHHHHHHHH!'**

She does it all the time but mostly when she's angry. Today she bit my finger really hard – when I tried to remove it from her mouth, she got really mad, shouted **'GAHHHH!'** and then punched me in the face!

I mean, does she just expect me to allow my finger to be bitten?!

I complained about it to Mum, and she just said, 'OOOOH, poor little Bella! She's probably teething and in a lot of pain.'

I wonder if when I get my braces and I'm in a lot of pain I'll be allowed to go around biting and hitting people too? As far as I can see, being a baby is a massive get-out-of-jail-free card.

MONDAY 30 MAY

My parents always get a bit wistful on bank holidays.
Apparently before we were all born they used to spend
them having lie-ins and brunches and long, lazy
afternoons at the pub. Now they have 5 a.m. wake-up
calls, pooey nappies and a house full of Lego.

I'm not sure what they want us to do about it. Are we
meant to feel sorry for them or something? No one
forced them to have children.

I had a look at my mum's Facebook page this morning
and it's literally just her complaining about how difficult
it is having children. I don't think she considers how
hard it is for me to be the daughter of a woman who
thinks it's funny to post 'wine o'clock' memes every
other day.

TUESDAY 31 MAY

Picture the scene: me and Jess, lying on my bed watching TikToks and eating KitKat Chunkys with the curtains closed (that is pretty much my perfect day, incidentally) and then Mum comes in and starts going off on one for absolutely no reason!

'It's a beautiful day out there, girls! You are going to rot your brain cells by watching that rubbish in the dark. Please get outside and do something!'

'OMG, Mum, it's half-term! We are trying to relax and enjoy a brief respite from the incredibly stressful experience of school.'

'The incredibly stressful experience of school?! You don't know you're born. Wait till you're grown up and have children and proper responsibilities of your own. I don't think you fully understand just how much we do for you!'

Oh God, not this again.

'Don't worry, Mrs B. Me and Lottie were actually about to go out for a jog!' said Jess.

'Were we?'

'Yes . . . we were going to start the Couch to 5K . . . Remember?'

'Er . . . no.'

'Well, I think that sounds like an excellent idea. Well done, Jess,' Mum said, looking satisfied as she left the room.

'What did you say that for?!'

'Because it might actually be fun. We could be the next Paula Radcliffe!'

'Who's she?' I asked.

'She's a person who's famous for being great at running marathons.'

'Hang on . . . one minute we are sitting on my bed and the next you are trying to make me run a marathon?'

'Well, small steps, Lottie. We'll start with a little 5K.'

'I guess that does sound sort of achievable . . .'

'Great, now lend me a pair of trackie Bs and let's get going.'

I got out my faded Nike joggers for her, and we downloaded the app to our phones and set off.

It was all going really well until we ran past the bakery and the smell of fresh doughnuts and iced buns stopped us dead in our tracks.

'We could just take a teeny-tiny break to refuel?' suggested Jess.

'Yeh, it has been about twenty-five minutes since our last KitKat Chunky.'

'Exactly.'

So we accidentally ordered a sausage roll and a doughnut each and then . . . well, it's very difficult to eat while running so we went home and ate them on the sofa.

Anyway, we did do the Couch to 5K of sorts . . . but just the opposite way round.

'Well, I do feel pretty good after that run. I'm fitter than I thought,' I said to Jess.

Jess was like: 'Lottie, we got as far as the bakery round the corner. We literally ran for about two hundred metres.'

Oops.

WEDNESDAY I JUNE

7.35 a.m.

Today is the biggest day of my life!

BOWLING WITH BOYS DAY!!

I am very glad that Molly will be there with me though –
when it's just me and her, it seems like old times. It's
only when Amber muscles in that things get tricky. But
not today – there is no way that Amber gets to worm her
way into our bowling date.

10.45 a.m.

You know what I just said? **IGNORE IT.**

You will not believe what just happened. (Or actually you
probably will, as you know what Amber is like by now.)

WhatsApp convo with Molly:

MOLLY: You know we are going bowling today?

ME: Yeh, I was aware.

MOLLY: Well, you know Amber just got together with Laurence?

ME: I was aware of that also.

MOLLY: Well, she asked if they could come bowling with us and I kinda maybe said yes.

ME: Did you kinda maybe say yes, or did you just say yes?

MOLLY: I just said yes. Sorry.

ME: 😒

MOLLY: But come on, Lottie – it'll be fun! TRIPLE DATE – YAY!

ME: YAY.

I said yay in capital letters but really it's a miniscule yay.
Or a not-at-all yay because **URGH!** I really do not want to
go on a triple date with Amber!

7.45 p.m.

Dad dropped me off at the bowling alley at three
o'clock and I walked in with my head held high. I was
determined not to let my confidence or bowling skills
ruin my date. Sure, Amber was there, but that didn't
mean that me and Daniel couldn't have fun anyway.

I could already see all the others at the lane. Amber was
inputting everyone's names into the computer.

'Oh great, Lottie's here!' she said. 'I'm giving everyone
bowling nicknames. What would you like yours to be?
Hang on – is that a booger in your nose?'

My hand shot up to my nose to check . . . but I didn't feel
a thing.

'You must have got it – it's gone now! Anyway, that gives
me an idea for your nickname, LOL!'

I looked up at the board and I couldn't believe what she had input me as!

'Hey, that's not very nice! How come everyone else has cool names except me?'

'Oh, chill, Lottie – it's just a joke,' Amber said, laughing.

'Soooo funny,' I said sarcastically.

I didn't really care though; I knew she was trying to wind me up and it wasn't going to work.

Not today, Amber. **NOT TODAY!**

I could see Daniel rolling his eyes behind her and waving

me over. He greeted me with a little hug, and I noticed that he smelt lovely and had not a trace of cheese powder under his fingernails.

'Hey, you. Ready to bowl?' he said.

'Let's do it!' I replied.

As I predicted, I was **TERRIBLE**.

On my first turn I scored zero and after three turns I was on 4 points and everyone else was over 25 – Theo was on 44! Fat lot of good those YouTube tutorials did.

Amber goes, 'Poor Lottie. Do you want us to put the gutter guard on for you?'

She really is an **ABSOLUTE COW BAG**!

For my fourth and fifth turn I scored zero, for my sixth turn I scored 2, for my seventh and eighth turns I scored 3, and for my ninth turn I scored **ANOTHER** zero.

It was just so unfair. Everyone else had got at least one

strike: Theo had four strikes, and Daniel and Molly had two.

I tried to put on a brave face, but it was obvious to everyone that I was starting to get upset.

'It doesn't matter, Lottie. It's just a bit of a laugh . . . No one cares who wins, do they?' said Daniel, trying to reassure me.

'Yeh, come on, Lotts. Don't get upset about it,' said Molly.

Laurence was up next, and he threw his ball into the gutter **TWICE**! Amber looked pretty annoyed with him. 'Laurence, did you do that on purpose to make Lottie feel better?'

OMG, was she for real?!

'No! I'm just pretty terrible at bowling.' He turned to me. 'At least we can be losers together, hey, Lottie?'

I grinned and Amber huffed. She clearly wanted Laurence to be as good as Theo or Daniel. I felt bad for him as he was actually a really lovely guy. Much too lovely for Amber anyway. It just doesn't seem right that she's so obviously using him.

For my final turn I was determined to get a strike and show them all that I wasn't quite as terrible as they thought. I was so far behind that I couldn't do anything to avoid coming last; it was more about saving at least a tiny bit of face.

I figured the ball I was using may have been too heavy so I picked up a 6 ball, gave it a discreet kiss, put my focused face on, took a big run-up and threw that ball **AS HARD AS I COULD**!

Unfortunately, because the ball was so light – and because I was obviously much more powerful than I gave myself credit for – the ball went flying and almost took out someone's nan in the next lane.

'Oh my God, are you trying to kill somebody?' said Amber.

I felt my face flush with embarrassment.

'Look, Lottie! At least you got a strike,' said Daniel.

I turned round and, sure enough, I had knocked down all the pins . . . yes, it was in somebody else's lane but details, details.

Everyone started doubling over in fits of laughter and Laurence gave me a high-five.

Then the manager came over, looking pretty cross. He said if we didn't stop messing about, we would have to leave. I tried to apologize and explain it was an accident, but I'm not sure he believed me. By that point we were all starving anyway, and it was obvious that Theo had already won with his unbeatable score of 144, so we decided to go and get dinner.

As we walked over to Pizza Hut, I felt Daniel's hand brush against my hand and then he casually wrapped his fingers round mine.

AAARRRGHH! We were holding hands!

AAARRRGHH! I was holding hands with a boy I like!!!!

AAARRRGHH!

I felt like I was in a movie or something. I looked around to see if anyone else had noticed. Amber was glaring at us, Laurence was standing behind her awkwardly, and Molly and Theo only had eyes for each other.

Pizza Hut was **DEEEELICIOUS**! M&D are so annoying and always try to get me to order from the children's menu, so it was great to have a proper adult-sized margherita with double pepperoni. Afterwards I said,

'Who fancies ice-cream factory?'

'OMG, Lottie. How old are you, like five? Ice-cream factory is for kids,' said Amber.

The others were shaking their heads too and my cheeks started to get hot again.

'Ha, look – she's going red!' said Theo, laughing.

'Theo! Don't be mean,' said Molly, elbowing him.

I could now feel my face changing from pink to scarlet.

Did you know that the absolute worst thing you can do to someone who is blushing is point out to everyone else that they are blushing – it makes the problem **ONE MILLION TIMES WORSE**.

'Sorry, Lottie,' offered Theo weakly.

'Hey, know what? I do feel like ice-cream factory after all!' said Daniel.

I can't quite describe how grateful I felt at that moment. Especially when everyone else started to agree.

'Me too,' said Molly.

'I'm in,' said Theo.

'And me – I actually love ice-cream factory!' said Laurence.

So, while the rest of us had fun being childish, making up the biggest, craziest concoctions we could, Amber sat there with a face like a slapped bum and ordered herself a cappuccino.

And do you know what? It was the funnest part of the day!

After we'd paid, the others went to play some games in the amusement arcade and Daniel and I waited outside. My dad was due to pick me up on the way back from collecting Toby from a party.

It was the first time we'd been left alone, and I suddenly felt really shy again.

'Well, that was fun,' I said, trying to break the silence.

'It was.'

'So . . .'

'So . . .'

We both laughed.

'Um, Lottie?' Daniel asked.

'Yeh?'

'I . . . um . . .'

He looked me in the eyes and then I thought: **OMG, HE'S ABOUT TO KISS ME!** And I totally panicked. I didn't know how to kiss . . . I needed to do some more in-depth research first and maybe practise on Teddy One-Eye or something. Or not Teddy One-Eye cos that would be weird. Sorry, Teddy!

'Daniel, I . . . erm . . . I . . .'

And just then I heard a huge **BEEEEEEEEEP** of a horn and a horribly familiar voice shouting at us . . .

Daniel looked terrified! He put his hands up in the air like he was about to get shot.

Why does this sort of thing always happen to me?!

'Dad, please!'

SO EMBARRASSING.

I checked the time on my phone crossly. 'Why are you always so early?'

'Thought the traffic might be bad,' Dad replied. 'Anyway, looks like I got here just in time,' he added with a raised eyebrow and a chuckle.

Now it was Daniel's turn to go bright red, and I wanted the ground to swallow me up at this point. But wait – it gets worse. Yes, honest.

Toby suddenly appeared behind Dad, wound down the window and shouted, 'OOOOOOOOOOOOHHH, LOTTIE'S GOT A BOYFRIEND!!!!!!!'

'Shut up, Toby!' I snapped.

'AND YOU WERE GOING TO KISS HIM!'

I said, 'SHUT UP, TOBY!'

He started making a kissy-face with such horrendous sound effects that I seriously wanted to cease to exist somehow.

'Dad, tell him to shut up!'

'Be quiet, Toby. Don't embarrass your sister in front of her date,' he said, laughing.

I could have killed the pair of them.

I started to walk over to the car, eager to get this horrific encounter over with. Unfortunately, Dad had other ideas . . .

'Hang on a minute, Lotts. Are you not going to introduce us to your boyfriend?'

I wanted to scream: 'HE'S NOT MY BOYFRIEND!'

'Fine. Dad, this is Daniel. Daniel, this is my dad.'

'Hi, Mr Brooks,' said Daniel nervously.

'Hi, Daniel. Good to meet you. I hope you weren't thinking about kissing my daughter?'

Daniel looked like he was about to throw up. 'No, I . . . errr . . . I wouldn't . . .'

'Don't worry, lad. Only messing with ya!'

'RIGHT! Let's go!' I said, opening the car door and getting in.

'Hey, what about me? Don't I get to say hi to your boyfriend too?' said Toby, laughing.

'NO!'

'Bye, Daniel!' I called from the window as we drove off. 'Sorry about . . . all . . . this.'

He waved and gave me a small smile.

Now I'm home, in my room, and I can't stop replaying it in my head. It was all going so well – how could my dad and my brother do that to me?! To top it all off they both thought it was super hilarious and laughed all the way home. I bet Daniel won't ever want to see me any more after this and then Amber will be delighted.

I have the worst dad and brother in the world. **FACT.**

8.12 p.m.

I have had no choice but to resurrect the Fort of Shame. However, this time I've had to call it the Fort of Mortification because what I'm feeling is way worse than shame.

I think I'm going to have to spend a lot of time in here, so I have made several upgrades . . .

Lottie's fort of Mortification

Snack bar

Blankets and pillow

Home cinema

I'm not gonna lie – it's actually pretty nice. If I ever escape this current state of mortification (unlikely) I might just stay in here anyway.

It's just soooo warm and cosy. It's making me feel pretty slee–

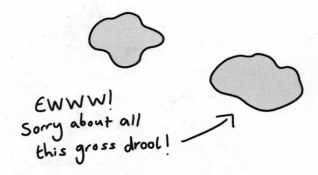

EWWW!
Sorry about all this gross drool!

THURSDAY 2 JUNE

Woke up in a mad panic! My phone was ringing, and my cheek was attached to my diary by my own saliva. I must have fallen asleep face first in it. My Fort of Mortification was obviously WAY too comfortable for its own good.

I looked at the screen – Daniel was FaceTiming me.

OMG!!!!!!!

I had fallen asleep in my spit, my hair was a state, I was still wearing yesterday's clothes and I was in a fort made out of blankets – could his timing be any worse?!

I quickly pulled the diary off my face and tried to smooth my hair down with my hands.

'ARGH! HELLO,' I said, answering the phone.

'Er, hi, Lottie. Why are you shouting?'

'Oh, I'm just a bit . . . confused. I've just woken up.'

'Sorry I woke you. Where are you? It looks really dark.'

'I'm . . . um . . . I'm . . . in a . . . cave?!'

OK, I know what you are thinking, but I panicked! I couldn't tell him that I was in a blanket fort, could I? It would make me sound like a toddler.

'A cave? But you said you'd just woken up.'

'Correct.'

'So . . . you slept in a cave?'

'Erm . . . kind of.'

'Why?'

Well, I don't know, do I, Daniel? I can't control the rubbish that comes out of my mouth . . . I mean, give a girl a break – I was asleep thirty seconds ago and my brain takes a while to warm up, OK!

I didn't say that though.

Instead, I just said nothing and then there was about thirty seconds of silence where both of us pondered what on earth I was going on about.

Luckily Daniel decided to give up on his cave interrogation. Phew.

'Anyway, I had a great time yesterday,' he said.

'Yeh, me too. It was lots of fun. Apart from the end bit. I'm so sorry about my dad and brother – they are so annoying!'

'Yeh, it was a bit embarrassing, but it's cool, honest. Plus, I was thinking – maybe they had a point . . .'

'What do you mean?'

He started looking super nervous. 'I mean . . . and you can say no, obviously, but . . . would you like me to be your boyfriend?'

'**WOULD I EVER!!!** Err . . . err . . . um . . . I mean that might be OK, I suppose.'

'Well . . . I suppose that makes you my girlfriend then?'

'I suppose it does!'

I was so excited that I just hung up without even saying goodbye and ran around my room shouting, 'OMG OMG OMG!'

I know I said I was trying to say OMG a lot less but TBH I'm finding it pretty hard. TBH I should probably start saying TBH less too. But TBH that's pretty difficult as well. OMG – shut up, Lottie!

Right, where were we? Oh yeh, I was OMGing about Daniel.

And then I thought, CALM DOWN, LOTTIE. *You've got to be casual about this or else everyone will think you are ~~weird~~ even weirder.*

So I had a lie-down on my bed . . .

But TBH (argh, I'm doing it again) that didn't really work either, so I decided to run downstairs and tell the fam the good news and apologize to Dad and Toby for being a bit mean yesterday because OMG (doh!), I have the best dad and brother in the world – **FACT**. (I know that's a bit opposite to what I said yesterday.)

They were all so happy for me and we all whooped and hugged and then one thing led to another and, before you knew it, we were all doing a conga round the house singing . . .

CONGA, CONGA, CONGA
LOTTIE'S GOT A BOYFRIEND!

THOUGHT OF THE DAY:

I'm starting to get quite concerned that my family is very, very odd. And yes, I do include myself in that.

FRIDAY 3 JUNE

My first full day of being a person who has a boyfriend!

Or being a girlfriend . . . as I guess that's the normal way to say it.

I feel like a proper adult. At least about nineteen or something like that. If you don't count the fact my dad has to do my school tie and I still can't use cutlery properly. Which I don't – because what is the point of ties and cutlery anyway?!

EXACTLY.

I dismantled my Fort of Mortification because who needs a Fort of Mortification when you have **A BOYFRIEND**?!

NOT ME!

Then I spent most of the day drifting about the house smiling. Dad kept going, 'Why do you have such a stupid look on your face, Lottie?'

How rude is that?

But my mood could not be dampened!

Even when Toby knocked on my door and called, 'Special delivery!' and left me a present outside my room, I did not react.

When he shouted, 'It's got a best-before date of next Saturday – after that it will start losing its potency!' . . . I just said, 'Thanks, Tobes! That's really . . . thoughtful of you.'

Because if my brother chooses to spend his time expelling body gas into empty jam jars it's of no consequence to me – like I say, I'm a proper adult now.

When Mum asked me to help bath Bella, I did it with a smile on my face and I actually enjoyed it. Bella can be so cute! At least until the part when she decided to poop in the water, which was quite frankly one of the most disgusting experiences of my life (second only to her actual birth).

You take over now, Mum. Sorry, but that is rancid!

How do you think I feel?!

GAAAHHH!

But, even with both of my siblings doing horrible things with their bottoms, I was still feeling as happy as Larry.

'You know, Lottie,' said Mum, 'I'm quite liking this new you!'

I said, 'Thanks – me too! Would you like me to stack the dishwasher?'

She nearly fainted!

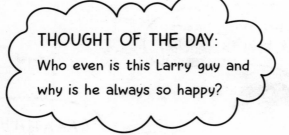

THOUGHT OF THE DAY:
Who even is this Larry guy and why is he always so happy?

SATURDAY 4 JUNE

Getting a bit worried about the kissing element of girlfriendom again.

I know I said I wouldn't do it, but I practised kissing Teddy One-Eye today.

Spoiler alert: it's a bad idea to kiss someone you have so much shared history with.

I don't think either of us liked it much and we agreed to never speak about it again.

SUNDAY 5 JUNE

I always hate the last day of the holidays because it means homework and I really HATE homework.

As if we don't do enough work at school! It feels super unfair that teachers ruin our weekends with it too.

Today's situation was bad because I had maths AND English AND history homework, but luckily Jess came over so we could do it together.

However, I was finding it difficult to be interested in anything other than Daniel.

Who cares about homework when you have a gorgeous **BOYFRIEND**?!

I'll give you a clue: not me.

It was just SO HARD to concentrate.

I mean, I was quite happy with the plan that Jess would do most of the work and then I would copy her answers, but she was less keen.

At one point I was just lying on my bed cuddling Teddy One-Eye, daydreaming about me and Daniel having a romantic walk on the beach, while Jess was trying to work out the cubic volume of a dodecahedron.

Then suddenly – whoosh! A big splash of water hit me in the face. Was it a wave?!?

I was drenched!

'What?! What's going on?!'

Jess was standing there looking angry, holding an empty glass.

'You did not just do that!' I said.

'I actually did just do that.'

'Why?!'

'We're meant to be doing our homework and you're just lying on your bed muttering to yourself like a crazy person!'

'Oh, so when you said you wanted to do homework together, you meant you *actually* wanted to do homework together?!'

'Er, yep.'

'So . . . then you threw a glass of water over me?!'

'I had no choice.'

'You did have a choice! It was entirely up to you whether to throw that glass of water at me. You could have just chosen NOT to throw it and IMO that would have been the better option.'

'Well, IMO throwing it was the better option! Lottie, we're meant to be doing our maths and you are not helping one bit. In fact, you are doing the opposite of helping because babbling about Daniel is just distracting me . . . so it's more like *anti-helping*.'

'*Anti-helping* isn't even a thing!'

'Whatever. Come on, Lottie. We need to get this done.'

It suddenly occurred to me that maybe Jess would be a bit less obsessed with homework if she had a boyfriend too.

'Do you like anyone at school, Jess?' I asked.

'I like plenty of people,' she said, sighing.

'You know what I mean. Is there anyone you **LIKE** like?'

'No.'

I could see her cheeks going pink, which was rare for Jess, as she never seems to get embarrassed.

'There must be someone? Come on – you can tell me!'

'Look, Lottie, there isn't – OK? Now are you going to help? This dodecahedron isn't going to work out its own volume, is it?'

WOW – I'd clearly touched a nerve. Why was she being so secretive about who she has a crush on?!

'Fine. Can you read out the question again then, please?'

'So the formula says that first we have to find the square root of five, which is . . .'

'Jess, do you think me and Daniel will end up getting married?'

'LOTTIE!!!!!!!!'

'OOOPS!'

This time I got a handful of Doritos thrown at me, which TBH was much better than water because I could eat them. Yum.

THOUGHT OF THE DAY:
Do you think me and Daniel will end up getting married though?!

MONDAY 6 JUNE

Back to school, which seems no way as bad as usual because now I have a **BOYFRIEND**!

Sorry, I know I may have mentioned that a *few* times already.

Me and Daniel held hands today at lunchtime and everyone stared. It took everything I had inside me not to keep saying, 'Yeh, this is my boyfriend . . . He's my boyfriend . . . Yep, that's right, this is me, Lottie Brooks . . . **WITH MY BOYFRIEND.**'

It probably would have been easier if I'd made a sign TBH . . .

TUESDAY 7 JUNE

I'm in trouble with Mr Peters because of the lack of maths homework. That makes four bad-behaviour marks, so if I get one more this term, I'm toast!

Jess refused to let me copy hers because she said that not being able to do homework because you are too busy daydreaming about boys is NOT a very good feministic quality. I fear she may be right, but I seem to be unable to stop myself.

I saw Daniel today in the corridor and he smiled and said hi to me, and I swear I melted into a pool on the floor and all that was left was a red hair bobble.

Then I forgot what lesson I was going to and ended up being five minutes late.

Is this what love does to you? Render you totally useless?

Oh crikey. Am I **ACTUALLY** falling in **ACTUAL** love?!

WEDNESDAY 8 JUNE

Oh great. Now I'm in trouble with Mrs Dodson for daydreaming in English.

Why, oh why can't people just be happy for me?!

I panicked that she was going to give me another bad-behaviour mark, so I told her I was finding it difficult to concentrate due to some personal issues I was having. Luckily she believed me – phew!

I think Jess is getting slightly annoyed with me as well. She keeps dropping some not-so-subtle hints that I talk about Daniel too much.

FYI she is still refusing to reveal who her crush is. She's pretty matey with Theo, so I've been wondering if it's him and because he's with Molly she obviously doesn't want to admit it.

THURSDAY 9 JUNE

Mr Peters announced in registration that Year Seven
would be going on an end-of-term trip to a place called
Treetop Adventures. If you've not heard of it before,
it's like an obstacle course up in the air with ladders,
crossings, climbing and zip wires.

The whole class whooped with joy – well, everyone
whooped except me.

You see, while I was glad of an excuse to be missing
lessons for the day, and trips out of school are always
fun, I am really scared of heights. And by 'really scared' I
mean *terrified*!

I've been invited to parties at Treetop Adventures before
and, as much as I've tried, I have never been able to
overcome my fear. I'll never forget the shame of Milly
Lewis's ninth birthday when I managed to make it up the
ladder to the start platform and then totally freaked out
and had to be carried down by one of the instructors.

CRINGE!

I'm twelve and a half now though and I've not attempted it again since, so maybe this time I will be OK. Here's hoping anyway!

Later on, I saw Daniel in science class.

'The trip's going to be great, isn't it, Lottie?'

'Errrr . . . yeh . . . really great.'

'Maybe we can sit together on the coach on the way there?'

Ooh, I hadn't thought of that. Suddenly the trip seemed a lot more appealing, because imagine sitting with my BOYFRIEND on the coach like proper grown-ups?! It would be INSANE! Maybe I could smuggle a bag of sweets on, and we could share them? Perhaps Maltesers . . . or no, maybe not Maltesers as they may go all melty. Maybe Tangfastics, but I guess some people don't like sour sweets, which is weird because I think sour sweets are **THE BEST**! I wonder if Daniel likes –

'Lottie . . . Lottie – are you still there?'

'What?!'

'I just said that maybe we could sit together on the coach, and you went into a sort of trance?'

'Sorry. Sorry. I'd actually love that,' I said, smiling.

'Great.'

'Um, Daniel – do you like Tangfastics by the way?'

'Yeh. **LOVE** them!'

EEEK! We are a match made in sour-sweet heaven!!!!!!!!!!!!!!

THOUGHT OF THE DAY:
After speaking to Daniel, I'm suddenly feeling a lot more confident about this trip. With him by my side, maybe I'll be brave enough to do it after all.

FRIDAY 10 JUNE

BIG NEWS! Daniel got me chips and
curry sauce at Frydays so our relationship is
clearly headed in the right direction. I let him pay
because I paid last time and I think that's OK.
Being a feminist would be very expensive otherwise.

We sat on a bench and ate them together. It was really
romantic, like that scene from *Lady and the Tramp* where
they eat the same strand of spaghetti and end up
accidentally kissing.

Except we didn't feed each other chips as that would
have been a bit gross and everyone would have laughed
at us . . . and we didn't end up kissing because – ARGH –
we've still not kissed yet, which is something that's been
playing on my mind.

Now we are officially a couple, I guess we should try the
whole kissing thing, right? But I still have no idea how to
do it!

SATURDAY 11 JUNE

Woke up absolutely freaking out.

I had the worst nightmare ever. I dreamt that me and Daniel had our first kiss and that I slobbered on him so much that his entire face was covered in drool.

It made me realize that I could have my first kiss ANY TIME and I need to be better prepared.

I thought about texting Molly because I assume she's probably kissed Theo by now, but I'm too afraid to ask her in case she tells Amber, who will then tell the **ENTIRE** school. It is exactly the kind of thing she would do.

HEY, EVERYONE! LOTTIE B IS THINKING OF HAVING HER FIRST KISS BUT SHE HAS <u>NO</u> CLUE HOW TO DO IT!!

10.23 a.m.

Had a brainwave to message my neighbour Liv. She is like the queen of cool and must have kissed loads of boys!

ME: SOS. I have an actual boyfriend now and I've no idea how to kiss. Any advice?!?

Can you really be an expert kisser at fourteen?! Apparently so.

（12.34 p.m.）

When I answered the door to Liv, she was clutching a big bowl of fruit – I was VERY suspicious!

We went upstairs to my room and sat down on the bed. 'So . . .' she said. 'Dating in Year Seven is pretty simple – you mostly just ignore each other, sometimes hold hands and possibly have a peck on the cheek or lips. There are of course more sophisticated kissing techniques –'

'WHOA! Stop there – no, thank you! I've seen kissing with tongues on the TV and it is **DISGUSTING**! I am NEVER doing that **EVER**!'

Liv laughed. 'Okaaaaaaay, we can discuss that again in a couple of years!'

Then she started laying out the fruit on my duvet cover.

'So, what are we doing . . . making fruit salad?'

'No, silly . . . We are learning to kiss . . . using fruit. Right, choose your weapon. You can pick whatever you like but IMO an apple or orange work well.'

'Okaaaaaaaaay,' I replied, unconvinced.

Liv sighed impatiently so I looked down at the selection and pointed at the mango (mostly because mmmm . . . I love mangoes).

'OK, good. Now pick it up.'

I picked up the mango.

'Now pretend you are on a date and you're having a nice chat.'

I looked at her blankly. 'I'm on a date with a mango?!'

'I don't have all day, Lottie. Do you want my help or not?'

'Um, I think I do . . . but I don't quite understand why –'

'Look, it's not a mango any more – it's a boy you really like. OK?'

'But what should I –'

'JUST TALK TO THE MANGO!'

Even though this was all absolutely bonkers, I didn't want to annoy her further, so I did just as she said.

So erm... do you have any hobbies?

'Right, better. Now you are moving closer and closer towards each other . . . You're finding the mango incredibly attractive . . .'

I promise you I tried to keep it inside, but I couldn't help a huge gulping laugh escape as I tried my hardest to find the mango attractive.

'Right, that's it. I'm going!'

'NO! Sorry, Liv. One more chance. I'm starting to feel it . . . The mango IS looking quite attractive. Maybe giving him a name would help?'

'Yeh, good idea. OK, the mango is no longer a mango. It's Barry.'

'BARRY?! I can't go on a date with a mango called Barry!?!'

'OK. Sorry – bad choice. That's my dad's mate from the angling club. It was just the first name that popped into my head. Anyway, I've got a better one . . . how about Antoine?'

'It's French?!'

'HE'S French. It's not a mango any more, remember. It's

a very good-looking French boy and he wants you to kiss him.'

'WOW – he's moving pretty fast, considering we've only just met. But OK.'

'Right, so, you are having a great date with Antoine, you maybe touch his arm or hand . . . I know he doesn't have any arms or hands, but if he did . . . Now gradually lean in, tilt your head to the side slightly and then BOOM – KISS THAT MANGO! Um . . . I mean . . . **KISS THAT HOT FRENCH DUDE**.'

So I did it. I leant in and I kissed Antoine.

My first Kiss*

* with a mango

Liv started clapping. 'That was amazing, Lottie! You've TOTALLY nailed it!'

'That's it?!'

'Yes, that's it – you are a natural!'

Wow, me – a natural kisser?! Who would have thunk it!

After that, Liv needed to go home for lunch, so we said goodbye. I watched her head downstairs. When she got to the front door, she turned round with a look of panic on her face and ran right back up again.

'I CAN'T BELIEVE I ALMOST FORGOT THE MOST IMPORTANT PART!'

'What? What did you forget?'

She grabbed me by the shoulders and looked me right in the eye. 'Lottie, you do not have to kiss Antoine or Daniel or anyone else if you don't want to. If you aren't feeling it, then just move away and say you don't feel comfortable doing that yet, or ever. And if he gets annoyed or sulky about it, then he's not worth a second more of your time or energy.'

Then she nodded her head as if agreeing with herself, turned and jumped back down the stairs three at a time.

I hope when I'm fourteen I'm just as wise as Liv.

(5.13 p.m.)

Fries Before Guys WhatsApp group:

> **ME:** I've spent the afternoon practising kissing!

> **POPPY:** You've kissed Daniel?! Wow this is MEGA!!!!!!!!!

> **JESS:** OMG!!!!!!!!!!!!!!!!!!!! We need details now!!!!!!!!

> **ME:** Blimey, enough with the exclamation marks. I don't mean Daniel.

> **ME:** I mean I've been kissing fruit.

ME: Or more specifically a mango . . .

ME: His name is Antoine.

ME: Hello? Is anyone still there?!

ME: Guys?

JESS: Sorry, just not quite sure what to say 😮

POPPY: Um . . . congratulations?! I hope you and Antoine will be very happy together 🤣

SUNDAY 12 JUNE

4.13 p.m.

Poppy popped over this afternoon. Ha!

I introduced her to Antoine and she agreed that he was quite good-looking for a piece of fruit.

I showed her my kissing technique and she thought it looked weird but OK, which is about as good as I could hope for. She suggested we make him more realistic by putting some of Toby's googly eyes on him, which I'll admit did help (sort of).

5.03 p.m.

Professor Barnaby Squeakington has started acting really strange around Antoine. He is standing at the side of the cage just staring at him!

The Professor is still staring. He has a sort of soppy look on his face and, if I didn't know any better, I'd say he was falling in love! Bonkers.

7.04 p.m.

Now he won't stop squawking. I think he's trying to talk to Antoine . . . OMG, maybe he's trying to ask him out?!?!

MONDAY 13 JUNE

I'm afraid I have bad news to share.

Antoine is no more. Mum ransacked my room looking for
dirty plates and glasses and also took my beloved mango.
She said he was going a bit soft so she decided to make
him into a smoothie.

I can't believe it. The first person – I mean mango – I'd
ever kissed, and he has been blended to death in her
Nutribullet!! What a grisly end. Poor, poor guy.

She couldn't understand what I was so upset about, and I certainly wasn't going to explain.

And, if you think I feel bad, you should see Professor Squeakington. He's devastated! He just lost the love of his life, and he can't stop thinking of all the things they were going to do together . . .

THOUGHT OF THE DAY:
What am I going to use to practise my kissing technique now?!

TUESDAY 14 JUNE

I've tried kissing a satsuma but it just isn't the same. You know what they say – you never forget your first kiss.

WEDNESDAY 15 JUNE

WARNING: Do not attempt to kiss a banana! It's **REALLY** weird.

You basically have two options and both of them are physically challenging.

If I had to pick one, I'd go with option two but only because option one resulted in a stalk to the eye, which was kinda painful.

THURSDAY 16 JUNE

Sat with Daniel at lunch. (We both had cheese paninis, which were extra melty and yummy today.)

He said, 'I've not seen you much this week. What have you been up to?'

'Yeh, I've been a bit busy,' I replied.

'Oh yeh? Doing what – homework?'

'Kinda.'

I obviously didn't want to tell him that my homework involved kissing various items of fruit.

FRIDAY 17 JUNE

SHOCK HORROR! Laurence has dumped Amber.

I mean, everyone could see she was just using him, but no one expected **HIM** to dump **HER**!

'So what happened?' I asked him in drama class.

'She expected me to follow her around all the time and it was getting really boring. I'll have much more time for Dungeons and Dragons Club now I don't have to do that any more. Plus, you know what?'

'What?'

'She wasn't even very nice to me. Once she said that I reminded her of a warthog.'

'Wow, that is mean. You don't look anything like a warthog!'

'Thanks. And, for what it's worth, you don't look anything like a blobfish.'

'Hang on . . . What?! She said I looked like a blobfish?'

'Oops . . . Sorry, Lottie.'

ARGH – that girl! She really is a piece of work.

Then at Frydays after school, apparently completely over Laurence already, she was flirting with a boy in Year Nine!! As if she'd have a chance with a Year Nine – does she not understand social hierarchies?!

The Year Nine's girlfriend comes over and throws a chip at Amber and says, 'Get your greasy, cheesy chip fingers off my boyfriend!'

Everyone started laughing and Amber started crying and stormed off home. I couldn't help but think that karma had a part to play there.

Daniel goes, 'I'm glad we don't have drama like that!' which made me grin.

Ooh, and we made a plan to go to Palace Pier next Saturday – just like the dream in my last diary, remember? Perhaps that would be a good time to have our first kiss. EEK!

THOUGHT OF THE DAY:
Do I really look like a blobfish?!

This one is me

This one is a blobfish

Oh God. I think I do a bit!!

SATURDAY 18 JUNE

WORST DAY EVER.

I know I say that a lot, but this really was a strong contender.

Mum took us into town to get a Father's Day present for Dad.

As soon as we got there, Toby dragged us all into the Lego store 'just for a look' and then spent about twenty minutes begging Mum to buy him the Star Wars Death Star that cost over £600.

He kept saying, 'Please, Mum! I'll pay you back!'

Considering he spends all his pocket money on Robux about 3.7 seconds after getting it, this was never going to happen!

I said, 'What are you going to pay her back with, Tobes?! Your bottled bottom gas?'

He was like, 'Yeh, great idea!!'

The boy is **TOTALLY DELUDED**.

When we'd finally managed to drag him out of the shop, we were all hungry, so we decided to get something to eat in the food court.

Unfortunately, when we were on the up escalator, I noticed Daniel and Theo coming towards us on the down escalator with their mates Ben and Tom.

My brain said *HIDE, LOTTIE, HIDE!* but we were trapped on the escalator and there was nowhere to go. There is something absolutely mortifying about seeing people you know from school when you are out with your parents, isn't there?! It makes you feel like a little kid.

I tried to duck down behind my mum, which maybe could have worked. Unluckily for me, old eagle eyes – Toby – clocked what was happening and decided to take **FULL** advantage of it.

Next thing I know, he's screaming, 'OOOOOOOH, LOOK,

LOTTIE! IT'S YOUR BOYFRIEND!!!!!!!'

Oh God, not this again!

He was so loud that even complete strangers were turning round and looking and laughing.

Then Daniel's mates all started laughing too, so it was just me and him in the middle of everything, flustered and bright red and wishing we were anywhere else but there.

'SHE WANTS TO KIIIIIIIISSSSSS HIM!' shouted Toby.

'Just shut up, Toby!' I hissed.

'SHE WANTS TO MAAAARRRRRRRRY HIM!'

I tried desperately to put my hand over his mouth, but he pushed it off.

'SHE'S BEEN KISSING SATSUMAS AND MANGOES TO PRACTISE FOR KISSING YOU!'

OMG – he must have been spying on me!

OMG!!!!!!!!!!!!!!!!

At this point, Mum decided to intervene. But not exactly in the way I had hoped. She told Toby to stop being silly and then she started hollering down the escalator, 'So, you are the famous Daniel! We've heard SO much about you!'

All his mates are almost doubled over laughing at the situation, but she just ploughs on regardless. 'Maybe you could come round to tea one day and meet the rest of the family properly? I do a lovely cottage pie, don't I, Lottie?'

I could not believe she was being SO embarrassing. Her cottage pie is the worst thing you have ever tasted in your life.

By now we were at the top of the escalator, and I couldn't bear to look back at Daniel's reaction, so I just sloped off towards McDonald's to bury my face in a big box of nuggets.

There was one good thing about the day though – we got Dad an excellent present that he is totally going to **LOVE**!

SUNDAY 19 JUNE
(FATHER'S DAY)

Me and Toby set our alarms to make Dad a fabulous
surprise brekkie.

Because cooking often feels quite long-winded and
boring, we came up with a genius plan to put everything
straight on a plate and microwave it – this also meant
way less washing-up. Bonus!

We made all his faves – sausages, bacon, eggs and beans
and they looked amazing . . . Well, apart from the eggs,
which were still a bit jellyish, and the sausages, which
may have been a *teeny-tiny* bit raw in the middle, and the
beans, which had a *slight* coating of green fur on them.
(Not our fault really – we could only find half an old can
at the back of the fridge, but we did scrape most of the
mould off.)

We wanted to let Dad have a bit of a lie-in, so we waited

until 7.01 a.m. and then we dragged him out of bed to give him his pressie . . .

Next, we served up breakfast and he spent about forty-five minutes eating it – probably because it was so delicious that he wanted to savour every mouthful! Toby got bored and ran off to play Minecraft, but I stayed there to chat and make sure he finished every . . . last . . . bite.

'Cheers for that, Lottie Pottie!' he said, as he finally put down his knife and fork. 'It was absolutely . . .'

He sort of trailed off there, probably struggling to find a word that adequately described my culinary talents.

'That's OK, Dad. I wanted to make today special to make sure you knew just how much you are appreciated.'

'Ahhhh, I do, love. I know you are growing up fast and you don't have much time for your dear ol' dad these days, especially now that you have a boyfriend, but don't forget about me completely, OK?'

'Daaaaaaaaaaaaad!' I said, blushing. 'I'll never forget you, silly . . .'

'Glad to hear it!' he said, giving me a kiss on top of my head (which he only just managed because he's not that much taller than me these days!).

6.12 p.m.

Oh no – poor Dad, he's been vomming in the toilet for the last hour, which is a real shame on Father's Day, bless him.

I really hope it wasn't down to our microwaved breakfast?! I told Toby that the sausages might need slightly longer than twenty seconds.

It's also a bit of a shame for me as after being nice to him all day (which was pretty exhausting) I was going to ask to borrow/have a tenner. I feel like if I ask him now though, it may not go down too well . . .

MONDAY 20 JUNE

Urgh – got into trouble for passing notes in maths, which was ludicrously unfair as I was only trying to find out which outfit my classmates preferred for my date on Saturday! I mean, are we not expected to have a life outside school?!?!

Also, technically it was quite a mathematical note because it involved a tally chart and some adding up – but Mr Peters was unwilling to listen to reason and gave me detention after school where he made me write down ALL my times tables. URGH.

My day got even worse when I got home because Mum said, 'Great news, Lottie! The dentist has had a cancellation and you can go get your braces fitted on Wednesday.'

Like, define 'great news', Mum! Because, from where I'm standing, the dentist is basically trying to ruin my life!

So I said, 'Oh, that's a shame because unfortunately I can't do Wednesday.'

'Yes, you can. I'll just call up school and say you have an appointment; it won't be a problem.'

'They really don't like it when you miss school for **ANY** reason.'

'Hmmm . . . you don't usually mind missing school . . . What's this *actually* about, Lottie?'

I had no choice but to level with her. 'I've literally just got my first-ever boyfriend and I REALLY don't want to get braces right now,' I said, then blushed massively because I knew she knew what I really meant.

Then she laughed and I got moody at her. 'MUM! It's not funny.'

'Sorry, Lottie, I didn't mean to laugh . . . but boys will come and go, and teeth are very important. You only get one set, remember?'

'I know but . . . it's just really bad timing.'

'It's never going to be good timing, so it's best to get it done as young as you can. I had braces when I was an adult and, trust me, that's even worse.'

I sighed. My fate is sealed and there is nothing I can do.

PS At least the braces news distracted Mum from asking why I was late home, so I didn't get in trouble about the detention – tee hee.

TUESDAY 21 JUNE

Sat with Daniel, Theo and Molly at lunch – we were all having lots of fun.

Well, everyone was having fun except for Amber, who sat there silently glaring at us the whole time. I say 'us' but it was largely me. It was almost as if she was willing her eyes to become laser beams so she could kill me with them.

Erm, could I at least eat my cheese panini before you laser me to death?!

After about ten minutes, she gives up on the ineffective glaring and goes for a super-sad look instead, coupled with a few loud sniffs and sighs. It wasn't long before she got everyone's attention.

'Are you OK, Amber?' asked Molly.

'Yeh. You know . . . it's just hard seeing you guys all together like this when it's only been a few days since . . . since . . . Laurence dumped me.' And with that she put her head in her hands and started (fake) crying.

'Oh God . . . I'm really sorry. I didn't think! You wanna go for a chat?' Molly said.

Amber nodded slowly.

'Guys, I'm going outside with Amber. I'll see you later, yeh?'

We all said goodbye and they linked arms and walked off, but not before Amber turned round and gave me a smug, satisfied look.

I **KNEW** she was faking it!

I mean, she didn't seem very upset about Laurence in the

chip shop on Friday, did she?!

She obviously can't bear that I'm hanging out with Molly more now that I'm with Daniel and Molly's with Theo. It's like she's totally forgotten that Molly was my friend first!

(5.05 p.m.)

More bad news!

Mum and Dad are really mad. School just phoned and told them that I had five bad-behaviour marks for late homework, passing notes in class, not concentrating, throwing stuff and – I can't believe they actually put this as a reason – 'doodling a strange picture of an anteater with a human head'.

So now Mum and Dad have come to the conclusion that having a boyfriend is distracting me from my schoolwork and they – how unbelievably unfair is this? – have grounded me for an ENTIRE WEEK!!!!!!

I tried to explain that the timings didn't work very well for me because I have a date at the weekend, but they didn't even care! There was no sympathy AT ALL. They are like people moving around doing things but with **NO HEARTS**. Basically zombies.

URGH.

They said that if I could spend the next week catching up on my schoolwork, then maybe they'd reconsider letting me go out with boys again.

If I'd have known Dad was going to be so mean today, I wouldn't have wasted my money* buying him that lovely Father's Day T-shirt.

*It was actually Mum's money, but whatever.

6.25 p.m.

WhatsApp conversation with Daniel:

> **ME:** Do you want Bad News 1 or Bad News 2?

188

DANIEL: Hmmm. Bad News 1 please!

ME: Bad News 1 is that I'm grounded for a week, so I won't be able to go to the pier on Sat.

DANIEL: Rubbish! Why are you grounded?

ME: Oh, just because school and my parents are like the Fun Police.

DANIEL: 😜 Don't worry – we can do it when you are free. What is Bad News 2?

ME: I'm getting braces fitted tomorrow. 😱

DANIEL: That's not bad news – I bet you'll look cute with braces! X

ME: 😊

WEDNESDAY 22 JUNE

8.45 a.m.

This is the last time I will see myself without braces for the foreseeable future, so I spent about half an hour gazing into the mirror. Farewell, wonky teeth. See you on the other side!

3.25 p.m.

Entire face aches.

In too much pain to write more.

Send help.

And KitKats.

Actually, I can't even eat KitKats so don't bother. This just gets worse and worse. ☹

Hungry but unable to eat.

Mum made sausage and chips for dinner, forgetting that I can't chew at the minute. **HMPH**.

It was torture watching Toby tuck into it, especially as he kept going, 'Mmmmmm, this is so good, Tinsel Teeth.' He's so immature and rude!

Mum rifled through the cupboard to find some soup but all she had was pea-and-ham and, I'm not joking, it looked like monster sick. **VOM**. I mean, honestly – she could have been better prepared.

5.50 p.m.

Mum came up with the ingenious idea of putting my sausage and chips in the blender. I was sceptical at first and it did look pretty gross, but it was a million times better than pea-and-ham soup!

Dessert was liquidized KitKat Chunky – also surprisingly good!

$$6.23 \text{ p.m.}$$

Expected a flurry of messages from my friends this evening to see how I am but no – absolutely zilch! Not even heard anything from Jess, Poppy or Daniel. I could have died, for all they know!

Fries Before Guys WhatsApp group:

> **ME:** Errrr, hello. Anyone there? Does nobody care that I've just been through some incredibly traumatic mouth torture today?

> **JESS:** Oh sorry, Lottie. I completely forgot! I was just watching *Is It Cake?* It was the episode where they had to make handbags out of cake and honestly YOU COULD NOT TELL.

> **ME:** Fascinating.

JESS. Yeh, it really was. Anyway, how did it go?

ME: Not great. Am in quite a lot of pain. Had to eat a liquidized dinner and Toby is calling me Tinsel Teeth.

POPPY: LOL Tinsel Teeth is a good nickname – v funny 🤣

ME: Personally, I'm not that keen . . .

POPPY: How about Brace Face then? Ooh or Magnet Mouth?

ME: Or maybe just my actual name . . . Lottie?!

JESS: I've always liked Tin Grin 😃

ME: Well, thanks, guys. I feel a lot better now 😒

THURSDAY 23 JUNE

8.13 a.m.

Having the day off school because I am still in a lot of pain. Mum said that going in would be a better distraction than sitting at home feeling sorry for myself, but I convinced her in the end.

You see, what Mum doesn't realize is that I rather enjoy feeling sorry for myself (as you might have noticed) and anyway my mouth still hurts too much to eat proper food, so if I did go to school I'd probably starve to death.

9.11 a.m.

I have googled good things to eat for people with braces and one of the top suggestions is ice cream – result!

We didn't have much in the freezer, so I've sent Mum and Bella out on a mission to buy some. I would have liked to have gone too, but I'm still feeling quite weak and delirious, so I thought it was best that I stay here.

I've now set myself up on the sofa with my duvet and my plan is mostly to watch YouTube all day.

3.25 p.m.

Breakfast – strawberry ice cream.

Mid-morning snack – mint choc chip.

Lunch 1 – salted caramel, fudge brownie and chocolate sauce.

Lunch 2 – raspberry ripple and cookie dough.

Mid-afternoon snack – strawberry, mint choc chip and salted caramel with a mixture of chocolate and strawberry sauce. (I was being too greedy – this was not good.)

If you are wondering why there is lunch 1 and lunch 2, it's just because some people like two lunches and that's absolutely fine – OK? Don't judge!

After yesterday I would have thought that Jess and Poppy would have upped their friendship game, but I've not heard anything from them **OR** Daniel again today, therefore I had no choice but to upload an attention-seeking sad-face Instagram story.

14 Likes
Braces = ouchy 😞
1 star ☆ do not recommend

#worstpainever
#canteveneatakitkatchunky
#wanttodie #noonecares
#poorme #tinsel teeth

😊 Love ya Babe! het better soon!
😊 Tinsel teeth - LOL 😆

5.45 p.m.

WhatsApp convo with Jess:

JESS: OMG, just saw your Insta story – you look terrible!!!!!

ME: Thanks 😕

JESS: Soz, but you did ask!

ME: Um, I don't think I did . . .

JESS: Oh yeh. Oops. How are the braces?

ME: Not great. I can't believe you didn't message to see how I am (again).

JESS: I just did!

ME: Only after my 😕 Instagram story!

JESS: Better late than never? 😆

ME: It's hardly a laughing matter, Jess. I mean, for all you know I could have died!

JESS: Has anyone ever died from getting braces?

ME: I don't know . . . Probably at least one person has. Anyway – that's not the point.

JESS: What is the point then?

ME:

JESS: I'm waiting.

ME:

JESS: Are you still there?

ME: Yes.

JESS: What's the point then?

ME: Look! Stop trying to confuse me. Tell me what's been happening at school.

JESS: OK well, where to start . . . Moaning Mia started going out with Boring Ben, Lacey broke up with DJ, apparently because he has weird thumbs? Lola and Leo got together – everyone thinks it's mostly because their names sound good together, rather than them ACTUALLY liking each other.

ME: They aren't wrong . . .

JESS: I know, right? Er, what else? Chloe got into trouble for throwing a ruler in Spanish – it hit Florence in the face, and she starts screaming 'I'M BLIND!!!!!' and going around the room bashing into things and laughing. Mr Sanchez sent them both to Mrs McCluskey's office and now they both have detention for a week. Oh, Burger Tom was sick in the hall outside our form room, and it had – surprise, surprise – BURGER in it. SO GROSS! I mean, does he actually eat ANYTHING other than burgers?!

ME: I really appreciate the detailed account, Jess. Just wondering though, did you see Daniel at all?

JESS: I nearly forgot the most important part! You won't believe this – they ran out of cheese paninis at lunchtime! Like COMPLETELY RAN OUT!!!! I was like 'What on earth are we meant to eat then?!' and the dinner lady suggested – get this – hot pot! I mean, is she insane?! Who eats school hot pot by choice? FGS there could be dead bodies in it??!

ME: Look, Jess, I'm not being rude, and this is all very interesting, but what I really want to know is what has Daniel been doing – and why hasn't he messaged me??

JESS: Didn't see him. Sorry.

ARGH!!!!!!!!!!!

BTW, in case you are wondering, Burger Tom is called Burger Tom because he's obsessed with burgers and he once ate five burgers at lunch break for a bet.

6.35 p.m.

The ice-cream diet had been really delicious today but by teatime I was really craving some solid food. I was about to suggest that maybe we could Deliveroo a Maccy D's or Domino's as a treat for me for being so brave, but unfortunately Mum had already started making fish pie for dinner. She thought it would be nice and soft in my mouth, forgetting that it's one of my least-favourite dinners of **ALL TIME**!

FYI the only dinners worse than it are cheesy broccoli and egg bake **(VOM)** and lamb and peach stew **(DOUBLE VOM)**.

Anyway, I made an excuse that I was so tired and woozy from the Calpol and neglect that I'd skip dinner and go to bed early. Little did she know that my **SECRET** plan was to eat my **SECRET** stash of KitKat Chunkys. (A much better dinner than fish pie, hee hee hee!)

However, I stupidly hadn't bargained on Mum coming up to check on me . . .

Now she is VERY cross. Not just about the dinner evasion but about the fact that I was 'clearly well enough to be at school' and how I had missed so much 'vital education'.

That was absolutely not true! At school I would have been learning stupid pointless stuff about decimal points and how people used to get their hands chopped off for stealing bread. Whereas at home I did an online quiz called 'What Type of Biscuit Are You?' and found out I'm most like a Jammie Dodger! Yum.

FRIDAY 24 JUNE

This is the **ACTUAL OFFICIAL WORST DAY OF MY LIFE**! Yes, yes, I know I've said that multiple times in my diaries . . . but I ACTUAL OFFICIAL mean it this time!

Firstly, when I walked into registration Amber goes 'Nice braces, Cheese Grater!', which, as far as braces-related nicknames go, I hate even more than the others.

Then WORST OF ALL: I have been dumped!!

I saw Daniel in science for the first time in a few days and he just completely ignored me. I had to spend the entire lesson trying to concentrate on not crying and wondering what on earth was going on. Unfortunately, my mission was unsuccessful, and I cried all over my diagram of the female reproductive system so **THANKS FOR THAT, DANIEL**.

Then, when I went to pack my things into my bag at the end of the lesson, I noticed a note in there. Daniel must have dropped it in on his way past.

I have taped it in for you below. It may be a little hard to read because I couldn't help crying all over that too.

DEAR LOTTIE,
I'M REALLY SORRY BUT I CAN'T GO
OUT WITH YOU ANY MORE.
IT'S BEEN FUN BUT UNFORTUNATELY
I LIKE SOMEONE ELSE RIGHT NOW.
IT'S NOT YOU, IT'S ME.
DANIEL

My head hit the desk with a thud. **WHY ME?!?!??!**

'OMG, what's wrong, Lottie?' said Jess.

'It's over. He's dumped me.'

'What do you mean? Who has dumped you?' said Poppy.

'Yeh, who are you talking about?' said Jess.

Were they purposely being dumb?! I mean, how many boyfriends do they think I have??!

'Who do you think?'

'OMG – **DANIEL?!**' said Poppy.

'But why on earth would he do that?' shrieked Jess.

I pushed the note across the desk towards them.

They read it quickly and I watched their expressions change from shock to fury.

'Right, that's it – he's dead meat!' said Jess, packing her things together hurriedly.

'**NO!** Guys, please. I don't want to cause a scene.'

'But . . . he needs to realize how stupid he's being! How could HE dump **YOU?!**' asked Poppy.

I tried to smile weakly, but I couldn't stop the sobs escaping instead.

'Lottie, are you OK?'

I raised my head off the desk and saw Amber and Molly peering down at me with concerned looks on their faces.

I quickly shoved the note back in my bag, as the last thing I wanted was Amber telling the whole school about it.

'Daniel dumped her,' Poppy blurted out.

'**POPPY!** She may not want everyone to know,' said Jess, hitting her on the arm.

'It's fine. Everyone will find out anyway,' I replied.

'Oh, Lottie, I'm really sorry to hear that,' said Molly, putting her arm round me.

'Ugh, he's such an idiot!' said Amber.

'Has he mentioned anything about it to you guys?' I asked between sobs. I wondered if they knew who this Someone Else was.

'No. He seemed a bit quiet when I've seen him lately, but I dunno,' said Molly.

'I wouldn't give it a second thought,' said Amber. 'It's his loss. Onwards and upwards, I say!'

Everyone murmured in agreement with her, and I was pretty shocked that even Amber was being nice to me – usually she'd be the first one to get a dig in. I appreciated them all supporting me and trying to make me feel better. But it didn't help that much, because all I could think was . . .

1. HE LIKES SOMEONE ELSE ?!?!

2. I'm deffo not eating a peperami for lunch again as it makes me do really smelly burps

← GROSS

I mean, what did I do wrong? Is it my embarrassing family? Is it the braces? Is it the fact he knows that I kissed a banana? Is it the Peperami-scented belching? Is it my general inability to act like a normal human being??

I guess TBF there are quite a few reasons he may have gone off me, but I thought he was different from other boys. I thought he liked me for **ME**.

And after everything we'd been through to get to where we are . . . did our crazy ice-cream creations mean NOTHING to him?!??!?

I can't believe I kissed all that fruit for him – what a massive **WASTE OF TIME**!

This is the worst pain ever!!!!!!!!

PS Still no cheese paninis in the canteen, which felt like the final nail in the coffin.

THOUGHT OF THE DAY:
Do you think he actually does like Someone Else or do you think that's just an excuse and he's dumped me because Amber is right and I do in fact look like a human cheese grater?!

Well, this is just grate!

SATURDAY 25 JUNE

Spent the morning in my room voluntarily doing my English homework. We have to write a poem that conveys an emotion of our choice. Mrs Dodson is right – poetry is much easier to write with a broken heart.

'Half a KitKat' by Lottie Brooks

She lies bereft on her bed.
Crumpled sheets, crumpled dreams.
Half of her heart is missing.
Too weak from crying to look at her phone,
Instagram stories left unwatched,
TikTok dances left unpractised.
She tries to eat a KitKat Chunky,
The chocolate mixes with the salt of her tears.
It's actually quite a nice combination . . .
But then the heartache starts again.
She can't finish it.
She folds the wrapper,

Saves the rest for later.

She's never not been able to finish a KitKat . . .

Maybe it's a metaphor?

Half a KitKat.

And only half a heart.

Decided to call Molly to try and find out something about this Someone Else Daniel was going on about.

'Hey, Lottie. What's up?'

'Oh, not much, just, you know . . . dying of a broken heart.'

'Oh yeh, I'm so sorry, babe. That totally sucks. Are you OK?'

'No. As I just said – I'm dying.'

'Cool. Well, apart from the dying, what have you been up to?'

IS SHE ACTUALLY LISTENING TO A WORD I'VE BEEN SAYING?!?

'Well, not much because all the dying is quite overwhelming, to be honest.'

'That's sad. Well, I was just planning my outfit for tonight because Theo is taking me to the cinema!'

Is she for real?

'How nice. Look, Molly, what I'm really phoning about is to find out if you know any more about the reason why Daniel split up with me. Do you think he likes someone else?'

'Oh, I don't know, babe. I'm really sorry. Hang on though. Amber's here – let me ask her.'

'NO! I don't want you to ask –'

'AMBER, DO YOU KNOW IF DANIEL LIKES SOMEONE ELSE? LOTTIE'S ON THE PHONE AND WANTS TO KNOW.'

OMG!!!!!!!

I can't believe she just asked Amber, who has like the biggest mouth in the entire world.

I can hear lots of muffled talking in the background and my heart starts beating really fast.

Finally, Molly comes back on. 'Amber said she saw Daniel on the way home yesterday and he said he didn't want to talk about it.'

There is more muffling in the background. 'Oh . . . and she reckons he still likes Marnie.'

Marnie – his ex-girlfriend – of course! It was as if someone just put a dagger through my heart.

'I mean, I could ask Theo about it tonight too?'

'NO! No, don't say anything. I don't want Daniel thinking I actually care.'

'You do care though . . .'

'*I* know that! But I don't want *him* to know that. I want him to think that I'm just going about having a GREAT LIFE and ABSOLUTELY NOT thinking about him. **EVER!**'

'OK, whatever you say, babe. I mean, no offence, but I'll probably get distracted by Theo's big brown eyes and totally forget anyway.'

'Errr, thanks . . . I think?!'

'You are **SO** welcome . . . Now if you had a cinema date tonight, would you wear jeans and trainers or dress up a bit more?'

I couldn't believe she was being so insensitive, so I just said, 'Jeans,' and got off the phone as quickly as possible.

9.35 p.m.

Mum came in, saw the half-eaten KitKat and immediately knew something serious was up.

I had no other choice – I told her everything and I felt a lot better afterwards.

Mum said she knew just what I needed – a girls' night in!

So we went out shopping and we bought ALL the chocolate and snacks we could carry. Then we ordered pizza for dinner, banished Dad, Toby and Bella from the lounge and watched cheesy Saturday-night TV together in our jammies.

And – although I spent half the night removing mozzarella, popcorn and Skittle sours that had got stuck in my wires (man, braces are annoying) – it was a really brilliant evening and EXACTLY what I needed.

Don't you just hate it that mums are always right?!

SUNDAY 26 JUNE

Nervous about seeing Daniel tomorrow, but if he's too much of a coward to dump me to my face, then I'm not going to give him the satisfaction of letting him know I'm bothered.

If I see him in the corridor, I am going to do the biggest laugh I can possibly do to show him how much fun I am having with him NOT IN MY LIFE!

Hopefully he is really regretting his decision by now and wishing he could turn back time. Well, sorry, Daniel, but it's TOO LATE! I've MOVED ON! I don't care about you any more and I NEVER WILL.

If he asks me to get back together with him, I will say **NO WAY** – he had his chance and he blew it!

HA HA HA!

THOUGHT OF THE DAY:

I lied.

I do care, I am bothered, I haven't moved on, and I would definitely get back together with him if he asked me.

I am officially the world's worst feminist! Hmph.

MONDAY 27 JUNE

Saw Daniel chatting to Theo in the corridor and before I
could execute my plan of doing a massive laugh to show
him that I don't care, HE did a massive laugh so now I
know that he doesn't care about me!

SO MAD!!!

The good news is that Mrs Dodson really liked my
poem. She said it was 'highly evocative' and that I have
a 'natural flair'. She also said that writing poems can

be incredibly therapeutic and helpful during traumatic times, so I thought I'd do another one for fun. What do you think?

'I Used to Really Like You' by Lottie Brooks

I used to really like you,
I thought you liked me too.
But now you like this 'Someone Else',
And I just feel like poo!

I mean, it may be a *little* juvenile, but I was pleased with the rhyming.

TUESDAY 28 JUNE

I found it difficult to motivate myself today. Even putting one foot in front of the other felt like hard work. It's like my entire body is just SO sad, from my head down to my toes.

It gave me an idea for another poem . . .

'Sad in the Toes' by Lottie Brooks

Sad in my heart,
Sad in my brain,
Sad in a car,
Sad in a train.
Sad in a bed,
Sad in a chair,
Sad in the face,
Sad in the hair.
Sad in the sun,
Sad in the snow,
Sad in the nose,
Sad in the toes.

This one is a toe (not a bin)

I'm getting pretty good, aren't I?!

One good thing to come out of this excruciating heartbreak is that it might help launch my career as a professional poet.

THOUGHT OF THE DAY:
Do you think hair can technically be sad, considering it's actually just dead cells?

I'm a strand of hair and I get really sad when I think about my BFF Lucy who got snipped off in a haircut.

WEDNESDAY 29 JUNE

I think people are starting to lose interest in my suffering.

Today is the fifth day of no cheese paninis at school and it's all Jess and Poppy could talk about. They had absolutely **ZERO** interest in hearing about my poor sad hair/toes.

Then when I got home I was wandering around with a dramatic miserable face, hoping to get some sympathy from MY OWN MOTHER and she goes, 'This is getting a bit silly now, Lottie. You can't mope about forever!'

So I went to my room to have a heart-to-heart with my hammies, but even they looked totally disinterested.

Oh well. At least their collective lack of sympathy has inspired another poem . . .

'Nobody Cares' by Lottie Brooks

The hamsters still turn on their wheel,
The mother still noisily hoovers,
The father still hides in his man cave,
The brother still farts and laughs about it,
The baby still tries to claw people's eyes out for fun,
The friends still keep banging on about
    cheese-panini shortages,
And all the while . . .
The boy she likes, likes Someone Else.
And EVERYBODY thinks there are bigger things in
    the world going on,
Like global warming.
Which admittedly is a bigger thing.
But some things aren't bigger . . .
Like hoovering, farting and a lack of cheese paninis.
And other people should remember that!

If I keep on like this, I'll probably have enough for an anthology soon.

THURSDAY 30 JUNE

Jess arrived unannounced after dinner to check up on me. I was lying in bed surrounded by pages and pages of my heartbreak poems.

'What on earth are you doing, Lottie?' she said.

'Writing poetry.'

'Why are you writing poetry?'

'Because that's what sad people do. When I have enough poems, I'm going to send them to a publisher and see if I can get a book deal. I have five finished now so I only need another ninety-five. Hopefully I can finish by the end of the weekend.'

She picks one up
and starts
to read . . .

Never again

We'll never again
eat chips and curry
sauce.
We'll never again
ride along the beach
on a horse.

'Lottie, I don't want to sound mean . . . but these are . . .
ABSOLUTELY AWFUL!'

'That's pretty rude!'

'Well, what are you even on about . . . ? When did you
and Daniel ever ride along the beach on a horse?!'

'It's called poetic licence, Jess! And also . . . it was hard to
think of anything else that rhymed with sauce.'

'Well, sorry, but if you are going to be a poet you need to
get used to accepting criticism. What are you going to
call this anthology anyway?'

'The working title is I Thought You Liked Me and Now All I
Do is Cry. What do you think?'

'Erm . . . cheerful! Can I suggest an alternative?'

'Yeh.'

'I Thought You Liked Me, but You Were Just an Idiot and I'm Too Busy Going Out for Bubble Tea with My BFF to Cry. See You Later, LOSER!'

I couldn't help but laugh. 'It might be a bit long, Jess.'

'I'm sure the editor will help cut it down when you get your publishing deal. Now come on – there's a raspberry with apple popping-bobba tea with your name on it and I'm buying!'

I collected up the pages of paper, got out of bed, pulled on my jeans, ran a brush through my hair and followed Jess downstairs.

She was right – the poem anthology could be finished later, and bubble tea turned out to be just the distraction I needed.

As we were sipping our drinks (so yummy!), I realized I owed her an apology.

'Thanks for this, Jess,' I told her. 'And I'm sorry if I've been a bit boy-obsessed lately . . . and a *teeny* bit dramatic about the whole Daniel thing.'

'Oh . . . you reckon?!' she said, grinning.

I snorted and nudged her with my elbow.

'You'll get it one day, Jess – just wait until you get together with a boy you REALLY like, and he suddenly dumps you for no reason!'

She looked down shyly and slurped the remainder of her drink through her straw, clearly hoping I'd change the subject, but, er . . . that wasn't going to happen . . .

'I knew it – you TOTALLY like someone!'

'I don't.'

'You so do! Every time I mention boys you start blushing. Come on, Jess, I won't tell anyone . . . I swear!'

'I said I don't like anyone, Lottie. Just leave it!'

'OK . . . OK . . . I was only asking. Jeez!'

'Whatever. I've got to get back – it's nearly dinner time.'

She was clearly getting annoyed, so we debated the pros and cons of bubble tea versus frappa-whappa-thingalings all the way home – a much safer subject.

THOUGHT OF THE DAY:
I don't get it . . . Why is Jess acting so weird whenever I mention boys? It's obvious she REALLY likes someone – but WHO?!?! I'm totally going to make it my mission to find out!

FRIDAY 1 JULY

At lunchtime Jess and Poppy came running up to me in a panic. 'Lottie! There are still no cheese paninis and people are starting to get scared and confused. I know you're going through a difficult time, but you need to get your priorities straight!'

They were right. This was just the wake-up call I needed!

We needed a plan of action, and most importantly we needed to temporarily change the name of our WhatsApp group!

SATURDAY 2 JULY

We Love Cheese Paninis (and Feminism)! WhatsApp group:

> **POPPY:** Hi, Cheese-Panini Lovers – it's been seven days since we last ate a cheese panini. I repeat – SEVEN ENTIRE DAYS! Our fellow pupils are suffering – they are hungry, they are weak, and they are finding it hard to concentrate in lessons. Tia fainted in geography yesterday! We need to hold a school protest before someone gets seriously ill!

> **JESS:** Great plan! I was thinking that we could protest about a feminist cause at the same time so that people take us a bit more seriously. What do you think?

ME: Good idea. Sorry if this is a stupid question though, but what have cheese paninis got to do with feminism?

JESS: It's our given right as females to have proper access to cheese paninis when we need them.

POPPY: But there isn't a shortage of cheese paninis just for females, Jess. No one is getting cheese paninis at all, are they?

JESS: Well, yes. But they are both important issues so we can still protest about them together.

POPPY: Even though they have nothing to do with each other?

JESS: Yes. All we need are some good slogans and no one will really notice that it doesn't make any sense.

ME: Okaaaaaaaay.

JESS: Great, well, glad that's sorted. We'll do the protest on Monday, so come to mine this afternoon at 2 p.m. and we can make the placards – OK?

POPPY: Sure thing! x

ME: See ya there. xx

(**8.24 p.m.**)

Just got back from Jess's.

I think we're all still a bit confused about what we are actually protesting about, but the placards look really great and that's the most important thing, right?

MONDAY 4 JULY

We arrived at school at 7.30 a.m. so that we could set up the protest, which was an error because, seeing as it was just the three of us holding placards, nothing really needed setting up (so we just looked at our phones for thirty minutes instead).

At 8 a.m. the first teachers and pupils started to arrive, so we stood up and started chanting and waving our placards around – people seemed quite impressed!

When the canteen opened at 12.20 there was an abundance of cheese paninis and we were all hailed as heroes!

In the interests of full disclosure, apparently the catering company delivered them at 8.15 this morning in the middle of our protest, so it was actually a complete waste of time, but we all agreed there was no need to make our fellow classmates aware of this minor detail.

Jess asked one of the dinner ladies why the paninis had been AWOL for so long and she said that they had 'just made a mistake on the order forms'.

All that suffering and effort because someone didn't fill out a form properly – **HOW ANNOYING!!**

Still at least we can change the name of our beloved WhatsApp group back to 'Fries Before Guys' now.

FRIDAY 8 JULY

5.22 p.m.

Jess came round after school, and we were sitting in my room chatting. I was telling her about how I was going to have a break from boys for a while and she was like, 'Yeh, yeh, I've heard that before!'

I thought perhaps I'd have another go at finding out who her super-secret crush was and this time I wasn't going to be brushed off so easily.

'Sooooo. Are you ready to tell me who you like, Jess? Because I know there must be someone . . .'

She looked thoughtful for a moment, like she was finally going to tell me, but then she just said, 'Hmmm, not really.'

'What, no one at all?'

'Nah.'

'I thought maybe you like Theo . . .'

'Don't be silly! He's just a mate and anyway – he's with Molly.'

'What about Ben? He's always smiling at you in science. I'm sure he has a thing for you.'

She shook her head. 'I'm not interested in Ben.'

'Well, who then? Come on – there MUST be someone!' I said, giving her a little nudge.

She sighed and looked a bit frustrated. 'Well . . . I mean, if I'm honest I don't know if I even like boys like *that*.'

'What do you mean?'

Jess bit her lip nervously. 'It's just. I dunno . . . Maybe I like . . . girls more instead.'

I was shocked. I hadn't expected that at all. I had no idea
how to respond so I just said nothing, and then when the
silence grew awkward I did the worst thing ever –
I laughed. I don't know why – it must have been my
nerves or something.

Jess obviously thought I was laughing at her and, before
I could explain, she picked her hoodie up and ran out of
my room and down the stairs. I wanted to go after her,
but my body was frozen.

I heard the front door slam shut and she was gone, and
now I'm in my room feeling terrible and wondering

why on earth I laughed when my best friend told me something so important.

9.12 p.m.

When Mum came up to tuck me in (yes, I know you might think I'm a bit too old to get tucked in and maybe you are right, but I don't care – I like it, OK), I decided to speak to her about it.

'Mum, I think I've made a big mistake,' I said.

'I'm sure it's not as bad as you think, Lottie. What did you do?'

'When Jess came round today, she told me something big and I . . . I'm so ashamed . . . I just laughed.' My eyes filled with tears, thinking how much I'd let her down.

'Oh, darling. Don't cry – we can fix this. I know exactly why you laughed. Sometimes when we don't know how to deal with situations, our emotions can come out wrong. You just need to apologize and explain that to her, OK?'

'Do you really think?'

'I *know*! Go round and speak to her tomorrow. You are a good friend, Lottie. She'll understand you didn't mean it.'

I really hope she's right.

SATURDAY 9 JULY

First thing I did when I woke up was send Jess a message asking if we could meet up in the park. I wanted to apologize in person rather than over WhatsApp as it felt bigger than that.

The thing is that was nearly 1.5 hours ago, and she's still not replied. Now I'm really stressing that she's super mad and will never forgive me.

I could absolutely kick myself for being so stupid and insensitive.

12.35 p.m.

Dad made fish-finger sandwiches for lunch, but I only managed about two mouthfuls because my tummy felt so wishy-washy.

This is so much worse than all the times I was waiting for Daniel to message me. Jess is my absolute best friend in the whole world – what will I do if I lose her?!

2.14 p.m.

I've still heard nothing, and I started feeling quite anxious and panicky.

Luckily, Mum came to the rescue again. She gave me a hug and helped me slow down my breathing, then she said that she would give me a lift to Jess's as it was important to sort this all out right now.

We are stopping at Sainsbury's on the way, because I have a plan and need some supplies.

Please keep everything crossed that it works and Jess forgives me!

5.55 p.m.

BIG RELIEF!

When we got to Jess's, Mum waited in the car while I knocked on the door. I felt weird turning up uninvited, but Mum was right – it was important that I explain things properly.

Roxanne, Jess's mum, opened the door and was followed by a waft of her amazing Caribbean cooking.

'Lottie! It's so good to see you,' she said, which I was glad about as I wasn't sure whether Jess would have told her what had happened.

'Hi, Roxanne. Good to see you too. Something smells nice!'

'I'm making your favourite – jerk chicken. Will you stay for dinner?'

'Um, thank you . . . I'm not sure . . . I just popped by to see if Jess was in . . .'

'Well, you'd be very welcome,' she said, then she turned and hollered up the stairs: 'JESSSS! LOTTIE'S HERE!'

241

Just then I felt some warm squishy arms wrap themselves round my legs.

'Ottie uddles?'

I grinned down at Jess's baby sister, Florence, and then picked her up and gave her a big squeeze. She immediately grabbed my ponytail and started yanking it and laughing.

'Oww, not too hard, Little Miss Trouble!' I said, spotting Jess coming down the stairs.

'Come on, you. Leave Lottie alone and come and help Mummy with the rice and peas,' said Roxanne, lifting Florence out of my arms.

'Hi, Lottie,' Jess said, leaning against the door frame and giving me a small smile.

I took a deep breath. My stomach was full of knots. I didn't want to get it wrong again, but I always find it so hard to get the words out right.

'Jess, I . . . Sorry to just . . . turn up, but you didn't reply to my message and . . . I've been so worried! Jess . . . I really wan–'

'WHOA! Hold up. I didn't reply because I've not even switched on my phone yet. I've had my cousins and auntie here this morning and, unlike SOME people, I am not attached to my phone 24/7.'

'OMG, I'm SO relieved . . . You're not mad with me?'

'Of course I'm not mad . . . Has anyone ever told you that you need to stop being so dramatic?'

I laughed. 'Maybe a few people.'

I was SO glad to hear her say that, but at the same time I knew I still owed her an apology.

'I'm really sorry about yesterday, Jess.'

'You don't need to be sorry. Everything is fine.'

'It's not fine though. You told me something important and I laughed. I don't know why, and I wish I could take it back but it just . . . just . . . came out so wrong.'

She smiled. 'I get it. I was kind of shocked I'd said it too. I'd never even said it out loud before. But I knew you weren't really laughing at me. It was silly of me to run off like that. I guess I panicked a bit too.'

You won't believe how good it felt to hear this. I hadn't totally messed things up – she understood!

'Oh, phew, I'm so glad! Because whether you like girls or boys it doesn't change anything – you know that, right? You'll **ALWAYS** be my BFF!' I told her.

'Thanks, Lottie, that means a lot.'

'And did you know that I have gay aunties and they are the coolest aunties ever!'

She laughed. 'I'm not sure if I'm gay or not yet. The way I see it is that I still have plenty of time to figure it all out.'

'Totally.'

'And, Jess?' I said after a minute or two.

'Yes?'

'Thanks . . . you know . . . for telling me.'

'That's OK.'

We fell silent for a moment and then she clocked the Sainsbury's bag at my feet.

'What's in there?' she asked.

'Oh . . . not much – just a bottle of Diet Coke . . . and some Mentos.'

'OMG OMG, are we gonna do a Mentos explosion?'

'WE SURE ARE!'

She put on her trainers, and we waved goodbye to

Roxanne and Florence, and to Mum in the car, then we headed over to the park, arm in arm. It was like a massive weight had been lifted. I made a promise to myself that I'd never let her down again.

MONDAY 11 JULY

Today is Bella's six-month birthday and we had a little party to celebrate. I thought it was rather unfair as me and Toby don't get half-birthday parties, but Mum and Dad told us that we did when we were babies.

Bella is now old enough to eat food, which people seem excited about – I'm not sure why. Mum is doing something called 'baby-led weaning', which basically means giving Bella chunks of food to throw around the room.

I suggested spoon-feeding would be quite a lot easier, but it seems that Mum prefers the throwing method. I also suggested that the spoon-feeding may ensure more of the food gets inside the actual baby as opposed to all over the cupboards but apparently she prefers it this way.

Go figure!

Dad also announced our holiday plans – we're going to the South of France! I'm so excited as we've not been abroad for years. We usually go somewhere in the UK and we usually choose the week when it rains **EVERY** day. This summer I might actually get a suntan – wahooo!!!!!

WEDNESDAY 13 JULY

Eek! In trouble with the Fun Police again!

They have been checking in on my canteen-spending again, which is basically like stalking.

Mum goes, 'Lottie, I put thirty pounds in your account last week and there is only thirty pence left – what on earth have you been spending so much money on?'

'I don't know . . . I can only assume someone must have hacked my account.'

'They'd need to have hacked your thumbprint to do that . . .'

'Yes . . . I've heard rumours of a thumbprint-cloning machine in operation at school, to be honest with you . . .'

'Right, OK, so let me get this straight – your explanation for spending nearly thirty pounds in a week is that someone has cloned your thumbprint?'

'That's exactly right, Mother.'

'Fine, well, I'll obviously need to report this to the school, so why don't we have a little look and see what this thumbprint hacker has been buying . . .'

'NO! No need to do that . . .'

I can't believe school make it so that parents can see exactly what you are buying – it's a massive invasion of privacy!

'Wow, well, this is interesting . . . five cheese paninis, three slices of pizza, three bags of popcorn, four waffles, five slushies, two cheese scones, two bags of crisps . . . Shall I go on?'

'No. I think it's clear that the thumbprint hacker needs to eat more fruit and veg, and if I find out who it is I'll be sure to inform them.'

'You do that, Lottie. And you can also inform them that if

they can't be trusted to eat a sensible diet, then they will be having packed lunches every day.'

'You want to make packed lunches for the person who has hacked my thumbprint? Wow, that's awfully nice of you!'

She tilted her head to one side and gave me her *I'm warning you* look.

Dammit. I think she's on to me.

FRIDAY 15 JULY

FUMING!!!

Went to Frydays after school with Jess and Poppy.

We like to get there early if we can, so we don't have to queue.

We were already sitting on the grass, eating our chips, when Molly and Theo walked past. They both smiled and said hello, and then I did a double take because behind them were Amber and Daniel.

Amber goes, 'Hi, girls! How are the chips today?' and Daniel wouldn't even meet my eye.

Poppy mumbled that the chips were fine, and then they went over to join the queue.

'Did you see that?!' I said. 'Are they, you know . . . like, together?!'

'Noooooo, don't be silly!' said Jess.

'They did look kind of . . . close though,' said Poppy.

Jess whacked her. 'Daniel is Theo's friend and Amber is Molly's friend so naturally they are going to hang out sometimes.'

I tried to concentrate on eating my chips, just to give myself something else to focus on. But suddenly they didn't taste very good.

Before long, the group came out of the chippy and sat on a patch of grass a few metres away from us. I noticed with a heavy heart that there were only two packs of chips between the four of them. Once Daniel had unwrapped his, he offered them to Amber right away, and she giggled and made a big show of accepting.

'He's sharing his chips with her!' whispered Poppy with a horrified look on her face.

'But . . . he wouldn't . . . He can't like Amber . . . He wouldn't do that to Lottie!' said Jess.

'OMG, they are cheesy chips!' exclaimed Poppy.

I looked up to see Amber stab a particularly cheesy chip and I quickly turned away. This was pure torture.

'And he's got . . . I'm so sorry, Lottie . . . he's got . . . curry sauce as well!' said Jess.

I suddenly felt like I was going to be sick. I stood up, dumped my remaining chips in the bin and started to walk off.

'Lottie, wait!' Jess and Poppy called.

But I couldn't stop the tears swimming in my eyes.

All I could think was: *How could he do this to me? How could Amber be his Someone Else?*

He knows what she's like and he knows how she's treated me in the past. I just can't wrap my head around it.

If there is one good thing that's come from this though, it's that I had a lucky escape. I clearly didn't know Daniel very well **AT ALL**.

SATURDAY 16 JULY

WhatsApp conversation with Liv:

LIV: Hey, not seen you for ages. How'd things go with that guy? Did you kiss him?

ME: Long story but no. He dumped me because he likes Someone Else and I'm pretty sure that's my best frenemy Amber! 🙁

LIV: Glad you didn't kiss him first. Imagine if you'd wasted your first kiss on that loser!

ME: True. Still hurts though. Got any tips on how to get over a broken heart?

LIV: YES!! I know just what you need.

ME: Oh yeh, what?

LIV: A break-up haircut!

ME: I like the sound of that

LIV: Trust me. You need a little boost of confidence, and a great haircut is just the answer.

ME: OK I'm in.

LIV: Excellent. I know the best place. It's my mum's mate's and I'm sure he'll do you a freebie, given the traumatic circumstances.

ME: Excellent. Thanks, Liv! x

SUNDAY 17 JULY

Liv messaged this morning to say she'd managed to blag me a last-minute cancellation for 11 a.m. Result! I met her outside the hair salon and she was clutching a huge pile of hair magazines with lots of folded-down pages.

'I have LOADS of ideas, Lottie. This is going to be **SO MUCH FUN**!'

I started to feel dead nervous. I usually wear my hair the same way all the time and I wasn't sure if I was ready for anything drastic.

I felt better when we walked inside though. It was a really fancy salon with huge mirrors, shiny polished surfaces, and spotlights.

The receptionist led me to a chair and put a gown on me, then she asked if I wanted anything to drink. I said I didn't have any money, but it turned out it was FREE, plus you even got biscuits!

AMAZING!

Then my hairdresser came over and introduced himself. 'Hello, darling. My name is Adrian and I'll be cutting your hair today. Do you have any ideas as to what you would like?'

'Not really, probably ju–' I started to say.

'Yes, we do!' interrupted Liv, flicking through her mags. 'Something quite dramatic as she's just been through a pretty horrendous break-up.'

'Oh yes! Liv was telling me all about it . . . This Daniel boy sounds like a right idiot.'

I laughed. I liked Adrian already.

'Erm, not tooooo dramatic though,' I said. 'Maybe an inch or so off?'

'**WHAT?!** No, Lottie! That's just a boring trim. I was thinking . . . maybe a pixie cut like this one . . .' Liv pointed to a photo of a lady with a practically shaved head.

'NO!!! I still need to tie it back. Just a tiny bit off please, Adrian.'

'Leave it to me, ladies. I think we can give you a different look without taking too much off; maybe an angled bob with a shorter fringe. Trust me!'

I was taken over to get my hair washed and they had a massage chair to sit in with rollers going up and down in the back. I also got a proper head massage and it was so good that I nearly fell asleep.

Next Adrian combed my hair and started snipping away. Liv made him turn me away from the mirror so he could do a big reveal at the end, and I was kind of glad she did because **HOLY MOLY** was I surprised!

What do you think?

I couldn't believe the transformation. As I walked home, I felt like a model in a hair advert – I kept skipping and jumping about to make my hair swish around.

Unfortunately, because of all the swishing, I wasn't really looking where I was going and I walked face first into a lamp post. I felt a bit less like a hair model after that though, and a bit more like my usual awkward self.

MONDAY 18 JULY

OMG, I nearly didn't get to go on the trip! I got up early, took a shower and spent so long blow-drying my new hair that I almost missed the coach (which, as it turns out, may have been for the best anyway).

I ran most of the way to school and when I got there everyone was already on board. I took a brush out of my pocket and smoothed down my hair. I wanted it to look perfect for my entrance.

I climbed the stairs and then started to walk down the aisle towards my friends, swishing my new hair as I went (and keeping an eye out for stray lamp posts too, obvs).

I guess hair-swooshing might be a bit vain and shallow and not very feminist behaviour, but I never said I was perfect, did I?

I got lots of murmurs of appreciation until Mr Peters interrupted my moment in the spotlight to say, 'Lottie Brooks, you are late! Find a seat quickly and sit down. We need to get a move on!'

I guess he wasn't too keen on me using the aisle of the coach as a catwalk to show off my makeover – what a spoilsport!

I walked over to Jess and Poppy, but they were already sitting next to each other.

'Sorry, Lottie – we did try to save you a seat,' said Jess.

'Your hair looks **AMAZING** though!' said Poppy.

'Thanks. Don't worry, guys.'

I didn't have a seat, but at least my hair looked good – I guess you can't have everything?!

Unfortunately, there were no spare seats around them either. My eyes fell to the back row where I clocked Molly, Theo, Daniel and Amber.

'Hey, Lottie!' said Molly, waving. 'Love the hair!'

The rest of them carried on chatting and ignored me. Daniel didn't even look up – I made all this effort for him (sorry, I mean for *myself*) and he hadn't even noticed. ARGH, what was the point?!

I scanned the coach to find a seat and started to feel my nerves creep in. Everyone I knew had already paired up, so I was going to be completely on my own. I looked like a total Lottie No Mates and it was all my own stupid fault for messing about with my hair for so long.

'MISS BROOKS!' shouted Mr Peters. 'Stop dawdling and find a seat – **NOW!**'

I sighed and walked back up to the front of the bus. NO ONE with any sense sits at the front of the bus – it's reserved exclusively for the teachers and the pukers.

'You can sit here if you like?'

I turned and saw Burger Tom patting the seat next to him.

'Thanks,' I said, reluctantly noticing that he had a stack of brown paper bags on his lap.

'They're just in case,' he said. 'I don't really get travel sick . . . not much anyway . . . just . . . now and again.'

Wow. How reassuring.

The journey to Treetop Adventures was only forty-five minutes long, so I crossed my fingers that Tom would make it. And that he hadn't had burgers for breakfast.

Dear reader, he did not make it (in the worst possible way).

After about five minutes Tom started going white, after ten minutes he started going grey, and after fifteen minutes he had turned **COMPLETELY GREEN**.

'Are you OK?' I asked.

'I don't feel well,' he said weakly.

I quickly put my hand up. 'MR PETERS! MR PETERS! Burger Tom . . . I mean, Tom doesn't feel well!'

Mr Peters sighed. 'We are nearly there, Tom, and we don't have time to stop. We're already running behind schedule due to the late arrival of *certain* pupils.'

Then he went back to his sudoku puzzle book.

I looked out of the window, willing the bus to go as quickly as it could. Tom's nausea seemed to be rubbing off on me and suddenly I wasn't feeling great either. What did Mum always say the best thing to do was? Look at something stationary or look at something moving?

Beside me, Tom was now sweating and shaking. 'I think I'm going to be . . . I think I might be . . .'

'MR PETERS, I THINK HE'S GOING TO BE SICK!' I screamed.

Mr Peters turned round and looked at Tom, sighed again, then asked the driver to pull over. Luckily, we were heading past a service station and, as the coach pulled in, I breathed a sigh of relief.

That was until Tom stood up and, unable to hold it in a second longer, vomited right on top of my head.

All I could think was: **MY NEW HAIR IS TOTALLY RUINED** . . .

. . . before the smell worked its way deep inside my nostrils and I puked too – all over my own self.

why does this sort of thing always happen to me?!

The coach was suddenly filled with a mixture of laughter and squeals of disgust. I could hear Amber screaming, **'EWWWW, THAT IS SOOOOOOO GROSS!'** all the way from the back.

My throat burned with acid and my eyes filled with tears. I was absolutely covered. What on earth was I going to do?

Suddenly Jess and Poppy were by my side. Despite me being covered with vomit, they linked arms with me and helped me off the coach. When we were in the toilets, they used toilet roll to wipe the larger chunks of sick out of my hair and then washed it in the sink using hand soap.

'Oh my God, it's got bits of burger in it!' said Poppy.

'Hang on, that means he must eat burgers for breakfast too!' said Jess, looking totally disgusted.

Luckily, we had been asked to bring a change of clothes in case we got muddy, so I put on my spare T-shirt and jeans. Poppy had some deodorant in her bag, so she gave me a good blast with that too.

I mean, they were wrong. I looked like a complete mess and I smelt like dog food, but I honestly don't know what I would have done without them. They are the best friends ever.

We got back on the coach and Mr Peters had covered my and Burger Tom's seats in plastic bags. Everyone around us was holding their nose and I don't think I have ever felt so humiliated in my life – and that's saying something!

'Hey, Lottie,' shouted Amber. 'Wow, I love the new hairdo and that's a nice perfume you are wearing too – what's it called? Eau de burger?'

I wasn't in the mood for her silly games today. 'Oh, shut up, Amber!'

'Ooooh – someone's tired!' she said, smirking.

'I'm really sorry, Lottie,' Tom said as I sat down on the crinkly plastic.

He looked even more embarrassed than me. 'Don't worry – it's not your fault,' I told him. Because it wasn't really – he couldn't help getting travel sick. Although I guess he could stop eating quite so many burgers.

When we finally arrived at Treetop Adventures, Mr Peters said we needed to split into groups of five. He started reading out the groups from his notepad and I hoped so much that I would be with Poppy and Jess – but when their names were called out in group three, mine wasn't with them. *Could today get any worse?* I thought.

Yes – it turns out it could!

'Now – group four,' Mr Peters said. 'Molly, Daniel, Theo, Lottie and Burger Tom. I mean **TOM**!'

My heart sank.

'Mr Peters – I've had a hard day already . . .' I said. 'Please can I go with my friends?'

'Sorry, Lottie, but if I let you switch I'd have to let everybody switch. Plus, this isn't about being with your friends . . . It's a team-building activity, so working with people you don't usually spend time with is absolutely ideal.'

Yeh, about as ideal as having arms that are made of ham and being trapped in a cage with twenty-five hungry tigers! I thought.

I didn't say that out loud because I didn't want to get into trouble, but that's what I would have said if I hadn't already had five bad-behaviour marks this term.

What I said was, 'OK.'

I guess it could have been worse. At least I wasn't with Amber. TBH she looked pretty annoyed about being separated from her mates too.

Me and Burger Tom started walking over to join our group.

'Hey, Lotts – I'm so glad you're with us,' said Molly.

'Yeh, always good to have you, Cucumber Girl,' agreed Theo.

I smiled at them gratefully, while also noticing that Daniel was scuffing his shoes in the leaves and completely ignoring me. What was his problem?! Had he forgotten that he was the one who dumped me?!

I guess the anger at everything that had gone wrong already today gave me a burst of confidence because then I said really loudly, 'Are you sure you wouldn't have preferred to have **SOMEONE ELSE?**'

They all gave me a strange look and Daniel pretended to look really confused, even though he OBVIOUSLY knew what I meant.

Then it was time for the safety briefing.

'Right, everybody. I'm Mike and I'll be your guide on the course today,' said the instructor guy.

I looked up at the obstacles and that's when I remembered why it is called Treetop Adventures – because it really is right at the TOP of some of the tallest trees I've ever seen!

'I hope no one's afraid of heights,' Theo said, laughing as he put on his harness.

'You can't seriously expect us to climb up there? We could die!' I said to Mike.

'Don't worry – it's impossible to fall. We use double clips for everything, so you are always very safe,' he replied.

We lined up at the start of the course where there was a rope ladder to take us to the first obstacle. Daniel went first, without a hitch, followed by Burger Tom and Theo.

'You next,' said Molly.

I gulped. But I knew I had to give this a go. They wouldn't let us do it if it was dangerous and I had to admit it looked like it would be really fun . . . if only it was a bit lower down.

'Come on, Lottie. You can do this!' Molly said, obviously clocking my hesitation.

I took a deep breath, put my hands on the rungs and started climbing.

I'm not going to pretend that the next couple of hours weren't scary, but Molly helped me round each obstacle and I tried to keep focusing on what Mike had told us – it's 100 per cent safe.

Despite being terrified of heights and despite smelling of sicky burgers, I faced my fears and I did it! I mean, I may have taken about three times as long as the average person to complete it, but who cares?!

By the time we got to the end I felt elated. It was just the zip wire to go, and Theo said the zip wire was the funnest part, so I was almost looking forward to it. I say *almost* because it was also the highest part! But I shut my eyes tight and, before I could change my mind, I pushed off the side.

I may have embarrassed myself slightly on the way down . . .

But I did it and Theo was right – it was **SO MUCH FUN**!

I even landed elegantly and managed to keep my jeans clean. I couldn't believe it.

I unclipped myself from the harness and stood up to see that the rest of the group were clapping for me. Even Daniel. Weird.

I felt on top of the world! Mike said it was because of the adrenaline, a hormone that gets released by your body when you do something exciting or scary. Apparently it gives you a natural high and that's why he does skydiving. Crazy!

We walked over to the picnic tables to join the rest of the year group and have lunch. I was feeling pretty good about myself at this point TBH, and I think the universe must have realized I was being too cocky because the next thing I knew I had tripped over a log and landed face first in a massive pile of mud and leaves.

I was very grateful when Jess and Poppy ran over to help me up. I tried not to let it bother me. My hair was already ruined, so what difference did a few twigs and leaves make? But out of the corner of my eye I could see Amber pointing and laughing and, worse still, she was standing next to Daniel, who had also seen the whole thing.

I know deep down it doesn't matter what Daniel thinks of me any more. I might be clumsy and awkward and weird and, according to some, have an uncanny resemblance to a blobfish (thanks, Amber!) but I'm still proud of myself for today, and that's all that matters, right?

I suppose I'm still getting used to the feeling of being let down by someone who I thought liked me . . .

PS You'll be glad to know that Burger Tom wasn't sick on the way back to school, thank goodness. In fact, we spent the journey chatting and he shared his bag of bubblegum Squashies with me. Contrary to popular belief, he likes things other than burgers, and it turns out that we actually have quite a lot in common . . . what with our habits of getting silly nicknames and publicly embarrassing ourselves.

PPS Warning – Squashies, although very yummy, are **NOT** good for human cheese graters. I spent more time picking the remains out of my braces than actually eating them. #sadtimes

TUESDAY 19 JULY

I can't believe tomorrow is my last day at school!

I feel kind of emotional about it all, because a lot has happened in the last year . . .

- ★ Weeks survived at high school: 39

- ★ Times went bright red: 87

- ★ Nicknames: 9

- ★ Bad-behaviour marks: 11

- ★ Detentions: 4

- ★ Cheese paninis eaten: 116

- ★ Boyfriends: 1 (or 2 if you count Dan the Man – he does, but I don't)

- ★ New BFFs: 2

★ Times I have totally embarrassed myself:
errr . . . **WAY** too many to count!

When I first arrived at Kingswood High it felt MASSIVE
and I was so shy and scared, but now it doesn't feel that
big at all. Maybe that's because I feel bigger too, both
inside and out.

It's definitely been a journey and I feel proud of myself
for that. I can't help but feel a bit sad about how things
turned out with Daniel though, but maybe that just
wasn't meant to be. Anyway, enough of the sad chat
because today is a day for feeling happy and I have
plenty of stuff to feel grateful for, including . . .

1. Not smelling of vomit (last night's shower
   was one of the best I've ever had!).

2. Having lovely clean hair – free of sticks,
   mud and regurgitated burger.

3. Having the absolute best friends in the
   world.

4. Only one day left of school.

5. Six weeks of summer holidays!!!

6. NO MORE homework!

7. Last but definitely not least – being on the ground again.

WEDNESDAY 20 JULY

It's over – I'm done! The next time I set foot in school I'll be in Year Eight – an experienced secondary-school kid – and I'll be able to look down on the Year Sevens just as they did to me. It's a rite of passage and I can't wait!

No one did any work today. Classes mostly seemed to involve watching documentaries, gathering up our old work or colouring in. The teachers all looked really happy for once. No idea why!

Me and the girls mostly chatted about our summer holiday plans. Jess's grandparents are visiting from Jamaica and they are taking them on a trip to the Isle of Wight, Poppy is going to Vietnam to visit her aunties, uncles and cousins, Molly is off to Tuscany and I'm off to the Ardèche – how cultured and sophisticated we all are!

The only annoying thing is that the others are all away for weeks one and two and we are away for weeks three and four – so I will hardly see them until the end of the summer, sob sob.

This clash of schedules could have been easily avoided if Dad had consulted me first before booking. TBH I'd have preferred to stay in a private villa with a personal chef, lazy river, stables, tennis court, cinema room and spa, rather than camping, but when I mentioned that to the Fun Police, they did their Yawnsville 'We aren't made of money' speech again.

Anyway, even though it wasn't technically a Friday, everyone was still going to Frydays to celebrate the end of term and then eat chips on the green. It wasn't massively appealing to me though.

'I'm not sure if I want to go,' I said to the girls.

'What? Why not?' said Poppy.

I sighed. 'I just don't want to see Amber and Daniel together and I'd rather just hang out with you guys.'

'But you love those chips!'

'I know I do but sometimes I . . .'

'Look, Lottie, I'm going to level with you here,' said Jess. 'Are you a feminist?'

'Err. I guess so, yes.'

'Do you like eating chips?'

I smiled. 'Yes!'

'And what's our WhatsApp group called?

'It's called "Fries Before Guys".'

'Err, sorry, I don't think the people at the back heard you. I said, **WHAT'S OUR WHATSAPP GROUP CALLED?**'

'So . . . are you going to let a loser boy stand in the way of you and your chips?!'

'NO WAY!'

'Come on then,' said Poppy, laughing. 'Let's go before it gets too busy!'

When we got there, Frydays was heaving. We joined the queue and, even though I saw that Daniel and Amber were standing together again, I completely ignored them. (Or did really well at trying to ignore them – which was difficult as Amber has a voice like a foghorn!)

They ordered first and stood to the side while they waited for their chips. I was trying not to look over, honestly, but out of the corner of my eye I saw her put her arm round him and giggle.

Poppy must have seen too as she whispered in my ear, 'Lottie, just ignore them.'

Then the serving guy calls out, 'Large cheesy chips with a battered sausage for Daniel!'

'Ooh yay, it's our order, babe!' said Amber, squeezing his arm.

And suddenly everything became clear in my head. If Daniel wants to choose **HER** over **ME**, then he's an idiot and not worth a second more of my brain space.

So I march up to the counter, clear my throat and in front of everyone I go . . .

Daniel and Amber just stood there looking dead shocked and Jess and Poppy whooped and high-fived me.

Then I walked off with my two brilliant friends, eating chips and laughing, and it felt so good!

So that was my last-ever day as a Year Seven at Kingswood and it ended on a massive high. I started there with zero friends and, although I'm certainly far from the most popular kid, I know I've made two lifelong friends in Jess and Poppy.

On Friday we are all going to go shopping in town because we need new sunnies, bikinis and flip-flops so we can look super cool on our holidays.

I'm gutted they are both going away on Saturday though. I'm really going to miss them. But, when I get back from France, we are going to have the best summer ever!

THURSDAY 21 JULY

11.45 a.m.

First day of the hols, the sun is shining, and I'm feeling full of the joys of singledom.

No more boyfriends for me!

NO WAY.

Single like a Pringle and NOT ready to mingle!

I'm an independent potato snack!

I certainly don't need a boyfriend to make me feel good about myself. In fact, from where I'm standing (full disclosure: I'm actually sitting), boys just cause trouble.

So I'll buy my own chips and my own ice-cream factory and my own 99p McChicken Sandwiches because I'm a self-sufficient feminist and it feels **SO GOOD**!!!!!!!!!!!!!

. . . well, technically Mum will probably buy them, but you get what I mean.

From now on it's going to be me, myself and I.*

*Correction: me, myself, Fuzzball the 3rd and Professor Squeakington!

8.45 p.m.

Went to get my jammies on for bed and a WhatsApp popped up on my phone. I went to check it and I almost dropped my phone in shock to see who it was from!

> **DANIEL:** Hey, Lottie. Just wanted to say sorry I didn't get to say goodbye properly. And I'm sorry Amber was being mean to you (as usual). I don't know what she was up to yesterday. I know things have been a bit weird lately, but hoping we can be mates in Year 8? D.

OMG! I was NOT expecting that. I really didn't know how to respond. The way I saw it, I had three options:

1. Ignore it.

2. Reply with 'Hope you are happy with your new girlfriend, you big Wotsity-fingered meany – go away!' 😛

3. Be mature and rise above it.

I decided to go with option 3. After all, I will be turning thirteen in the not-too-distant future . . .

ME: Don't worry. No hard feelings. I can't pretend it didn't hurt to get that note but I'd like to be mates again too. L.

DANIEL: What note?

ME: The note you wrote me.

DANIEL: What do you mean? I never wrote you a note. You wrote me a note.

ME: I never wrote you a note!

DANIEL: Yeh, you did. You wrote me this . . .

> Dear Daniel,
> I'm really sorry but I can't go out with you any more.
> It's been fun but unfortunately I like someone else right now.
> Also you have Wotsity fingers which are off-putting.
> Lottie.

ME: OMG – no, I didn't!! But you wrote me this . . .

DEAR LOTTIE,
I'M REALLY SORRY BUT I CAN'T GO OUT WITH YOU ANY MORE.
IT'S BEEN FUN BUT UNFORTUNATELY I LIKE SOMEONE ELSE RIGHT NOW.
IT'S NOT YOU, IT'S ME!
DANIEL

DANIEL: I didn't write that, Lottie. I swear!

My mind was swimming – what on earth was going on?!

ME: So, someone sent you a note pretending to be me, and someone sent me a note pretending to be you?! But how come Molly never mentioned it to me when I asked her if she knew why you'd split up with me? Surely Theo would have told her about the note?

DANIEL: Theo didn't know anything about it. I was too embarrassed to tell anyone. I just told him things hadn't worked out between us.

ME: URGH. This sucks. Someone has totally tricked us!

DANIEL: Who would do something like that though?

I sighed. There was only one person that I could think of. One person who was jealous of me and Daniel being together and jealous of the fact that we were getting closer to 'her friends' Molly and Theo.

Would she really do something as low as this though?!

ME: I mean, I don't know for sure, but my guess would be your girlfriend, Amber.

DANIEL: Errr . . . she's not my girlfriend!

ME: She isn't your Someone Else?

DANIEL: No way! I could never like Amber in that way, you know that. I only hang around with her because I'm mates with Theo.

ME: But yesterday . . . I saw you together in Frydays!

DANIEL: You know what she's like. She was playing games. She was probably just trying to get to you.

ME: OMG I thought you didn't want to go out with me because I was a weird banana-kissing human cheese grater!! I can't believe I've been so stupid!

DANIEL: LOL. You haven't. She fooled us both. I thought your Someone Else was Laurence . . . or Burger Tom.

ME: Laurence?! No, of course not. He's just a friend. And Burger Tom?! After what happened on the school trip?!?!?! I'll never be able to eat burgers again!

DANIEL:

DANIEL: So . . . if you haven't got a Someone Else and I haven't got a Someone Else . . . do you know what that means?

ME: That we should shoot Amber into space on a one-way mission to Mars?

DANIEL: Well, yes. But it also means that maybe we could hang out again? I mean . . . if my Wotsity fingers aren't too off-putting . . .

ME: Well, let's see . . . Will you share your cheesy chips with me?

DANIEL: For sure . . . I may even get you a battered sausage too!

ME: YAY! 😃 When can we hang out?

DANIEL: I'm off to Greece on holiday first thing tomorrow but I'll be back on 5 August, so see you then?

ME: Nooooooooo! I go to France for two weeks on the sixth!

DANIEL: That sucks! Have a great holiday though, and I'll see you when I get back x

ME: You too! X

DANIEL: Oh and FWIW I think your braces look really cute x

ME: 😃 ! X

OMG, I think I'm in love (again) and yeh, I know what I said earlier about being completely off boys . . . It just turned out I only meant that for like nine hours. But I'm only twelve and I don't know what I'm talking about half the time so gimme a break, OK?

FRIDAY 22 JULY

Last night I dreamt that me and Daniel went on a date to a Pringles factory – I seriously reckon it would be the best date ever.

They had a swimming pool full of Pringles and we were told we could eat as many as we liked! I managed to stuff my face with 3,429, which was a world record (so I think they regretted inviting me a bit).

Met the girls in town. It took all I had not to blurt out my news immediately, but I wanted to have a proper chat about it so I suggested going to get a drink before shopping. We had a five-minute debate over whether to get strawberry frappa-whappa-thingalings or bubble teas. The frappa-whappa-thingalings won two to one, mostly because me and Jess had OD'd on bubble teas lately. Poppy was a bit annoyed, but she'll get over it.

When we had sat down with our drinks, I told them that me and Daniel had made up and this was their reaction . . .

(I think my friends also need to stop saying OMG as much TBH.)

Next, I told them about the whole notes fiasco – they were properly **SHOCKED**!!

Poppy almost fainted. She used to be besties with Amber for years but even she couldn't believe that Amber would be as tricksy as that.

'How do you know it's definitely Amber though?' asked Jess.

'Hmm . . . I reckon I'm ninety-five per cent sure, but I can't prove anything, can I? If I confront her, then she'll probably just deny it.'

'Do you still have the note?' asked Poppy.

'Sure.' I took it out of my jeans pocket and uncrumpled it for the girls to see.

'She definitely wrote that,' said Poppy. 'I mean, you can tell she's tried to disguise it to make it look like it could have been Daniel, but I was at primary school with her for six years – I'd know that handwriting anywhere.'

'So, what are you going to do?' said Jess.

I chewed on my straw. 'I really don't know – but maybe I'll worry about it later, because right now we have shopping to do. Come on!'

We slurped the remains of our frappa-whappa-thingalings and hurried out, arm in arm.

First, we headed to H&M, then New Look, Pull&Bear, Zara and Sports Direct. All our faves.

It was so much fun. The only problem was, I wished I had more money as there were loads of cool things I wanted to buy.

I ended up getting a gorgeous neon-green bikini (it's a sporty-style one with a crop top as that's much more my thing), a couple of T-shirts and a vest top. Poppy got a blue bikini and a sundress, and Jess got a gorgeous polka-dot swimming costume, some denim shorts and some flip-flops. Oh, and we all got new sunnies and books to read while we are lounging by the pool. I can't wait to go away now – I'm going to look très cool!

After we'd finished shopping, Poppy invited us back to hers so we could try on everything we'd bought (again).

'I wonder if any of us will have a holiday romance . . .' said Poppy, posing in front of her bedroom mirror in her new dress and a bucket hat.

'Not me!' I laughed. 'Things have been complicated enough lately.'

'Jess – what about you? Beth in Eight Yellow has been to the Isle of Wight and she said there are loads of good-looking boys there.'

I looked at Jess nervously. She hadn't told Poppy about possibly . . . maybe . . . preferring girls. Should I say something? Should I try and change the subject? Just as I was about to attempt to rescue her, Jess picked up a pair of aviators, strode over to the mirror, put them on and said . . .

Sometimes I wonder if Jess might be the coolest person on the entire planet!

5.54 p.m.

Daniel's gone!

I was kind of hoping his plane would break down, but he messaged to say he was on the runway about to take off, so I can only assume that they are well on their way now.

The reality is sinking in that I won't see him for an **ENTIRE FOUR WEEKS**, and it feels like a lifetime.

Just as we had finally made up, we were cruelly ripped apart again, courtesy of EasyJet, and I'm left in a sort of limbo wondering whether we'll just be friends or whether we'll get back together as boyfriend and girlfriend again.

Jess also went away today, and Poppy and Molly go away first thing tomorrow so literally EVERYONE is on holiday at the minute apart from me. Oh, and Amber, but I'm hardly going to hang out with her, am I?!

Oh well, at least my hammies aren't going anywhere . . .

THOUGHT OF THE DAY:
Should I confront Amber about the notes
or just ignore them? I really can't figure
out what the best way to handle it would
be. I don't want to get into another fight
with her, but at the same time should she
be allowed to behave like this? Part of
me thinks it's my responsibility to call her
out on it.

SATURDAY 23 JULY

It's July, it's freezing, I'm wearing jeans and a sweatshirt, and Mum is thinking about putting the heating on – go figure! In comparison, Daniel has uploaded an Instagram picture of himself at his fancy Greek villa. The sky is blue, the pool is glistening, and he looks so gorgeous and happy.

29 Likes

I could get used to this! ☼

#Schoolsoutforsummer

10.18 a.m.

~~Should he be that happy though . . . is he not missing me?! Maybe he'll meet a lovely Greek girl and forget all about me.~~ 🙁

10.19 a.m.

Crossed out the above entry because I realized that wasn't a very feminist thought. If he does meet a lovely Greek girl and forget all about me, then GOOD FOR HIM!

Anyway, maybe I'll meet a lovely French boy and forget all about Daniel! Unlikely TBF because he is sooooooo lovely.

4.24 p.m.

WhatsApp message from Daniel:

> **DANIEL:** It's amazing here but very hot! Went on a boat trip and to a Greek taverna for lunch. Miss you x

ME: It's not amazing here and it's just started hailstorming. Watched a YouTube video about how to make pancakes that look like Justin Bieber and ate a Peperami. Miss you too! X

DANIEL: You're so funny. 😂

ME: I'm not trying to be!

DANIEL: That's the best part x

4.29 p.m.

Bum – I'm doing Peperami-flavoured burps again! I mean personally I don't mind them, but I just don't want other people to notice and then get another nickname like Salami Breath Girl or Stinky Burp Lottie.

Why do Peperamis have to be so delicious, dammit?!

MONDAY 25 JULY

Toby is at Kool Kidz Klub day camp this week. I don't
know how they get away with calling it that TBH;
every single word is spelt incorrectly. How are kids ever
supposed to learn to spell properly when this is what
they are up against?

I used to go to Kool Kidz Klub when I was younger, but
it's for five- to eleven-year-olds and I'm now too old,
thank goodness.

I'm not going to lie – it's lovely and peaceful without him.
Plus, I don't have to worry about getting farted on or
finding his bottled bottom gas stashed about the house.

I slept in until 10 a.m. and it probably would have been
even longer if Bella's GAHHHing hadn't woken me up.

11.45 a.m.

Spent over an hour doing my hair and make-up for no reason whatsoever.

The end result was utterly fantastic, and I don't think I'd ever seen myself looking so good, which was pretty annoying, considering all my friends are away so there is no one around to appreciate my efforts.

I mean, if a tree falls in the woods and there is no one there to hear it, does it make a sound?

3 p.m.

Just back from town. Didn't really do anything, just went to sort of stand in the middle of the shopping centre in the hope that someone would see me and be all like, **'WHOA, LOTTIE, YOU LOOK AMAZEBALLS!'**

Unfortunately, the only person I recognized was Burger Tom and we are still both finding it a little difficult to

look each other in the eye since . . . well, since . . . you
know what!!

THOUGHT OF THE DAY:
If Lottie looks incredible in the shopping
centre but there is no one there to see
her, does she actually look that good?

TUESDAY 26 JULY

Had a really busy day today:

- ★ Woke up at 11 a.m.

- ★ Ate two bowls of Frosties.

- ★ Watched TV for an hour.

- ★ Ate a bag of Quavers.

- ★ Watched YouTube for two hours.

- ★ Ate cheese on toast.

- ★ Felt tired so had a lie-down.

- ★ Ate two bags of Monster Munch (one Pickled Onion and one Flamin' Hot).

- ★ Thought about getting dressed.

- ★ Didn't get dressed, as what is the point?

★　Messed about on TikTok for two hours.

★　Chatted with my hamsters.

★　Felt sorry for myself about Daniel for fifteen
　　minutes.

★　Had a little cry.

★　Complained to Mum about how bored I was.

★　Ate a KitKat Chunky.

★　Complained to Mum about how bored I was
　　again.

★　Complained about how there was nothing
　　to eat.

★　Ate another KitKat Chunky.

★　Watched the Justin Bieber pancake video
　　again.

Then at the end of the day Mum goes, 'Lottie, you can't just sit around the house doing nothing all summer holiday.'

I was like, 'Are you having a laugh?! I've done **LOADS** today!'

Then she goes, 'All you've done is eat stuff, look at your phone and wander aimlessly around the house.'

'Well, I mean, I'm sorry if all my friends have gone on holiday and totally deserted me!'

'I understand that, but you may as well try and use the time productively!'

'Use my time productively to do what?!'

'Well, how about doing a jigsaw? Or you could write a story, do a crossword puzzle or tidy your room?'

Is she for real?!

WEDNESDAY 27 JULY

Decided to be helpful today so I spent the morning trying to make the Justin Bieber pancakes for a family breakfast.

Unfortunately, they came out looking a bit more like a terrifying Peppa Pig!

Still tasted good though. In fact, they were so delicious that I ate ~~a lot most~~ all of them myself (oops), but it is the thought that counts, right?

I thought Mum would be really impressed with me, but it seems not because she also expected me to clean up after myself too – unbelievable?!

In the afternoon I felt tired, so I had a relax on the sofa and very occasionally called out to her to bring me snacks. Apparently she had a problem with this too and when Dad got home she told him I'd been 'lazy and rude'. I guess she must have forgotten that I'd spent all morning sweating away in the kitchen.

Dad was really cross with me and said that if I can't come up with more productive ways to amuse myself, then I will have to go to Kool Kidz Klub with Toby. I think he has forgotten that it's only for primary-school kids, so I'm not scared!

THURSDAY 28 JULY

To get the Fun Police off my back I made a timetable of activities to show how productive I am actually being . . .

Lottie's Summer funtable

	Mon	Tue	Wed	Thur	Fri
Morning	YouTube	Sleeping	looking at phone	Daydream on floor	TikTok
Afternoon	Snacking	Telly	looking at phone	Complain about how hard my life is	Telly
Evening	TikTok	Deliveroo McDonald's	Snacks	online clothes shopping	lie on sofa (with phone)

What a busy sssssschedule!

(I regret drawing a snake on it as I really don't like snakes, but it was the only animal I could think of that would fit in the space.)

For some reason, they weren't very impressed?!

Mum goes, 'Lottie, this is really quite concerning. Take Monday, for example . . . you aren't doing anything but eating snacks and watching mindless drivel from online content creators.'

'Look, Mum – trust me,' I said. 'If you're twelve and three quarters, that's like **THE** perfect day.'

FRIDAY 29 JULY

10.32 a.m.

NEE NAW! NEE NAW! The Fun Police have decided to confiscate my phone to prove a point – so now I'm just lying on the floor in the hallway feeling sorry for myself.

12.34 p.m.

Been here for two hours now.

1.31 p.m.

No one seems in any way concerned that I've had nothing for lunch.

1.35 p.m.

I'll probably end up starving to death right here in the hallway.

(1.45 p.m.)

Have made myself a Pot Noodle and returned to my spot.

(2.19 p.m.)

Still here.

(2.22 p.m.)

Mum has just hoovered around me.

2.55 p.m.

I wonder what it's like to have parents who actually care about you?

3.02 p.m.

They really need to consider getting the hallway redecorated. It's getting incredibly tatty.

3.13 p.m.

A fly has just landed on my arm. He's quite cute . . . for a fly.

3.14 p.m.

I've decided to name him Gerry.

3.15 p.m.

Oh. Gerry has gone.

I kind of miss Gerry. He's the only one who has bothered with me today.

She wouldn't miss me if she knew I'd spent all morning eating dog poo!

4.45 p.m.

Toby came home and decided to use me as a human trampoline, which was fun. And by 'fun', I mean incredibly annoying and also painful.

5.38 p.m.

Dad came home and just stepped over me! I mean, I could be dead, for goodness' sake?! **DOES ANYBODY ACTUALLY CARE ABOUT ME AT ALL?!**

OMG. Absolutely fuming! Mum has booked me into Kool Kidz Klub next week!

I told her I was too old for it, and she said that they had agreed to let me attend because she had informed them that I was so sad and miserable at home on my own.

This is 120 per cent categorically **NOT TRUE!** I was having a wonderful time being miserable, thank you very much.

She also told them, and this is the worst part, that I wouldn't mind that the activities were aimed at younger kids because I'm incredibly immature for my age.

HOW RUDE!

SATURDAY 30 JULY

You won't believe this – I've just had a WhatsApp message
from Amber.

> **AMBER:** Hey, Lottie. How is your summer going?
> If you are free today, do you want to get a
> bubble tea or something later? XX

WHAT THE?! She's REALLY horrible to me at school, she
tried to completely sabotage me and Daniel, and now,
because all her other friends are on holiday, she suddenly
wants to hang out?!?

I was quite tempted to reply with something like, 'HA – no
way! I'd rather gouge my own eyeballs out with a spoon!'

But then again that might be slightly mean, plus I really
want to confront her about the notes, and perhaps with no
one else around, this will be the only opportunity I have to
get the truth out of her.

Hmmmmm.

10.36 a.m.

OK, so I've thought about it, and I've decided that I do want to get some answers from Amber. No – I NEED to get some answers. I don't want to go back to school in Year Eight with this weirdness hanging over me. We need to sort this out once and for all.

Wow, I sound like a brave knight going into battle saying that, don't I?!

I hope I can hold my nerve when I actually see her in person!

Anyway, I replied with this . . .

> **ME:** Summer going OK, thanks. Been mega busy but free to hang this arvo, yeh. Bubble tea shop at 2 p.m.?

> **AMBER:** GR8 see ya there

ME: OK, see ya there.

I couldn't bring myself to add a smiley or a kiss – although I didn't want to ask her about it over the phone, I also didn't want to be fake.

4.35 p.m.

Well, that was **WEIRD**! But I'm really glad I went.

It was quite awkward at the start. Usually if I'm seeing my mates, I would hug them or be like 'hey, cool, good to see you', but with Amber it wasn't really good to see her, because – as we know – she's an absolute cow bag.

We ordered our drinks and as it was a nice day we went to sit on a bench in the sun. I struggled to think of how to start the conversation, but luckily she broke the silence first.

'So, how's stuff?' she asked.

'Yeh, good,' I replied. 'Missing my mates though. It's annoying they all went away at the same time.'

'Tell me about it.'

'How's stuff with you?'

'Fine, I guess. My parents are working every day, so it's been a bit . . . boring.'

Oh God. She looked really sad.

'That must be kind of . . . lonely.'

'Yeh. It is a bit.'

I couldn't figure out how I was supposed to act. I was still really mad at her, but I felt sorry for her too.

'So, any gossip?' she asked, trying to change the subject.

'Yes, actually. Me and Daniel made up.'

I watched the colour drain from her face and she started fiddling with the lid of her cup – I knew then with 100 per cent certainty that it was Amber who wrote those notes.

I pulled mine out of my pocket and put it on the table in front of her.

'Someone sent both of us these . . .'

Her eyes flicked across the piece of paper; she could barely look at it.

'Well, that's pretty . . . mean,' she whispered.

I was going to have to spell it out.

'Poppy said that it's *your* handwriting?'

Silence.

'Did you write it, Amber?'

Then I noticed that she had tears in her eyes. She was trying to hold them back, but it was no good and they started streaming down her face.

'I'm sorry. I don't know why I did it. I just . . . I was . . . jealous, I guess. You were organizing these double dates and I felt like I was being left behind. It was so stupid – I wish I could take it back.'

I didn't know what to say. I had expected her to deny it. I hadn't expected her to just come clean like that. **AND** apologize – I mean, it was hardly very Amber!

'I can't pretend I'm not hurt. It was a pretty horrible thing to do – did you even think about how I would feel? Or how Daniel would feel?'

'I . . . I don't know what to say . . . I was so scared I was going to lose Molly as a friend. I'm so sorry, Lottie.'

And then she started properly sobbing and you won't believe this – my arm just sort of started levitating, like it had a mind of its own, and the next thing I knew it was round Amber's shoulder!

'Don't cry. It's OK. But listen – you don't need to do stuff like this . . . Molly's a good friend. She wouldn't just desert you.'

'I know, you're right. Please don't tell her, Lottie, please! She'd be so mad at me for hurting you that she might not forgive me!'

I sighed. I hated to see Amber upset like that and I understood how she was feeling. It's horrible to feel like you are being pushed out. I knew that only too well.

'I won't tell her, but you need to promise to start being nicer to me, OK?' I said as I nudged her affectionately in the ribs.

She wiped her tears away on the sleeve of her hoodie and smiled at me. 'I can try, but I can't promise,' she said with a wink.

I laughed. It did feel really good to clear the air.

She asked if I wanted to hang out next week and I had to admit I was off to Kool Kidz Klub, which she found totally hilarious. We agreed to sort something out with Molly, Jess and Poppy when I was back from holiday – I'm not sure I'm ready to be BFFs with her after everything that's happened, but I guess it would be cool if we could all get along.

THOUGHT OF THE DAY:

Sometimes I have to remind myself that Amber acts the way she does because she's feeling sad or insecure. It can't be easy for her being an only child whose parents work long hours. I'm going to make a real effort to try to understand her better.

I still can't believe I actually hugged her today though. Isn't life just MAD?!?!

MONDAY 1 AUGUST

I mean, I won't admit it to Mum, but Kool Kidz Klub
wasn't as bad as I thought it was going to be.

The good thing about little kids is that they look up to
older kids and actually listen to what you have to say
(instead of just hoovering around you).

TUESDAY 2 AUGUST

Today was **SUPERHEROES DAY**. Actually, I quite
enjoyed it.

You'll be pleased to know that we did find the Peace
Crystal, which we threw into the Volcano of Doom –
the volcanic reaction created Love Lava (which instead
of being molten hot and deadly was actually yummy
strawberry jam). Then everybody ate yummy jam
sandwiches and forgot about being evil and destroying
the world – hurrah!

Personally, I found the plot a little basic, but Lola wouldn't listen to any of my (better) ideas – she can be quite intimidating considering she's only in Year One.

I mean, Dr Nasty Face? Really?!??!

WEDNESDAY 3 AUGUST

Today was **SPORTS DAY** and I absolutely cleaned up!
I won the egg-and-spoon race, the long jump, the high
jump, the 100-metre sprint and I was instrumental in the
success of the 4 x 100-metre relay too.

Not naming any names, but some (most) of the kids got
a bit upset as they thought that by being older I had a
significant physical advantage. They were all like . . .
'Her legs are twice as long as mine' or 'Wahhhh – I'm
only five!'.

A few of them were even crying! I had to give them a bit
of a pep talk afterwards because, honestly, it was quite
pathetic.

Look, guys, you'll never get anywhere in life if you keep making excuses for yourselves!

THURSDAY 4 AUGUST

Today we made animals out of toilet rolls. It was great fun! I think Mum is right – maybe I am just incredibly immature for my age?!

Some came out better than others, but I think I like the elephant best . . .

FRIDAY 5 AUGUST

Today was my last day at Kool Kidz Klub. It was a bit
sad saying goodbye to all my new mates. I suggested
setting up a WhatsApp group to stay in touch, but then
I remembered they were all too young to have phones,
so we'll probably never see each other again – never
mind.

Speaking of phones, during circle time I heard mine
ping so I snuck off to check who it was, and it was a
message from Daniel!

DANIEL: Our flight's been moved so we'll be
back earlier than I thought. Should be home
at 5ish so could pop round for an hour and
say hi? x

ME: Yeh, that would be great!

DANIEL: Cool, see you then! How are you
anyway?

ME: Fine but we are about to start a game of Duck Duck Goose and it's my favourite, so chat later.

DANIEL: OK, good luck!

After Duck Duck Goose (which I was excellent at) I showed the gang my messages and they were dead excited for me.

I feel like I may actually burst with happiness when I see him! I'm a bit nervous about him coming to my actual house though. I have told my family to try to act as normal as they possibly can, but I'm not holding out a huge amount of hope.

SATURDAY 6 AUGUST

Had an emotional 'hi and goodbye' with Jess this
morning when I dropped the hamsters round for her
to look after. She had a great time on the Isle of Wight.
It sucks that we didn't have more time to catch up, but
I had to head home to get ready for our hols as we are
leaving v early in the morning.

Mum said that me and Toby were old enough to pack
our own suitcases now. Personally, having seen inside
Toby's suitcase, I think she's wrong because all that's in
it so far is a Super Soaker, two Nerf guns and seventy-six
bullets (he's counted), a pair of ski goggles, three tubs of
home-made slime, a three-foot cuddly Alsatian, a folder
containing his top 138 Match Attax cards (again, he's
counted), a vampire's cape, a fart gun and a plastic axe.
I asked him if he was thinking of taking any items of
actual clothing, and he said, 'Oh, yeh, good idea.' And he
blindly stuffed a handful of clothes in the case straight
out of the dirty laundry bin!

To his credit, he did take clean pants, but what concerned me most was the quantity.

'Toby, you know we are away for like two weeks?' I said.

'Yeh – why?'

'Well, you've only taken two pairs of pants . . .'

'Yep, that's because one pair of pants lasts eight days.'

I mean, I should have just removed myself from the conversation at this point but unfortunately my curiosity got the better of me.

'And how . . . exactly . . . does one pair of pants last eight days?'

'Well, duh! First day you wear them the normal way, second day you wear them front to back, third day you wear them inside out, fourth day you wear them inside out AND back to front, fifth day you start the entire process from the beginning with the same pair of pants and that takes you to day eight! On day nine, just as pair one are starting to smell a bit, you crack out your fresh pair!'

I really, really wish I hadn't asked.

I said, 'Toby, did you know that most people change their pants daily?'

'Yeh, well . . . most people are just stupid.'

I guess he has a point.

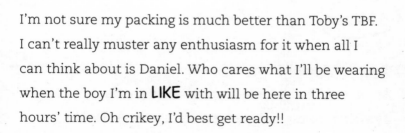

3.45 p.m.

I'm not sure my packing is much better than Toby's TBF. I can't really muster any enthusiasm for it when all I can think about is Daniel. Who cares what I'll be wearing when the boy I'm in **LIKE** with will be here in three hours' time. Oh crikey, I'd best get ready!!

5.05 p.m.

I had a shower and washed and dried my hair, then I applied strawberry lip gloss, peach blusher and two layers of mascara. Clotheswise, I am wearing frayed denim shorts and a Nike T-shirt and bare feet. It's a look that says: *this girl is so casual and carefree it hurts!*

It's a shame my face won't cooperate with the look

5.20 p.m.

Feel sick. I think I'm going to throw up. Which would be terrible as the last time I was in close proximity to Daniel I smelt of vomit and I don't want it to be **A THING**.

5.25 p.m.

Applied an extra layer of mascara – three for luck and all that!

5.29 p.m.

I think three layers was a bit OTT – my lashes feel clumped up and gummy. I wonder if those magnetic false eyelashes I keep seeing advertised on Instagram actually work?! **ARGH**, that's the doorbell – he's here!!

6.24 p.m.

Feeling very emotional.

I bundled Daniel straight into the garden as Mum and Dad started to ask him deeply intrusive questions such as, 'How was your holiday?'

Why do they always have to speak to my friends?! Don't they understand that kids don't want to be interrogated by strange, boring adults?

He looked even more gorgeous than usual. He was wearing a white T-shirt that made him look super tanned and he had these really cute freckles on his cheeks and nose. His hair's normally light brown but now the sunlight had streaked it blonde.

I felt SO shy. I think he was feeling the same way as we did quite a lot of awkward standing about and not really knowing what to say to each other and then he goes, 'Lottie, I got this for you. I thought you could wear it on holiday to remember me by.'

He pulled a small present out of his pocket and gave it to me. OMG, it was a really nice necklace with a sparkly diamond heart on the end! Apparently it's only plastic, not real diamond, because if it was real it would have cost about £300,000 instead of £2.50 – but I don't care. **I LOVE IT!**

Then for some reason I said, 'I've got something for you to remember me by too . . . I've, errr, just got to go into the house and . . . get it.'

It was a really stupid thing to say because I hadn't actually got him a present, so I ran about inside desperately trying to find ANYTHING to give him. In my panic I grabbed the toilet-roll elephant I'd made.

When I presented it to him, he said, 'This is for me to remember you by . . . a toilet roll?'

'It's not JUST a toilet roll!'

'Oh right . . . yeh . . . erm . . . is it a mouse?'

Personally, I felt like that was a bit rude because apart
from being grey it clearly didn't look anything like a mouse!

'Have you ever seen a mouse with a trunk? It's actually an
elephant.'

'Sorry, yeh, I see that now. It's . . . er . . .'

'A bit weird? Yeh . . . I know.'

'Nah, it's actually perfect to remember you by, Lottie,' he
said, laughing.

Then I laughed too and then he sort of shuffled towards me,
and I looked at him and he looked at me, and then there
was a bit more shuffling, and then suddenly we were holding
hands and I started thinking: **ARE WE GOING TO KISS?**

My heart was thumping and my legs felt really wibbly –
I'm not sure if I've ever felt quite so nervous. But it also

felt right, so I tried my best to relax. And then suddenly I felt his lips touch mine and I was weirdly calm again and all I could think was . . .

THIS IS IT! I AM HAVING MY FIRST KISS ON THIS BEAUTIFUL SUMMER'S EVENING WITH A BOY I LIKE. IT TASTES LIKE SUNSHINE, AND WATERMELON AND WEIRDLY ALSO. . . BBQ BEEF HULA HOOPS AND IT IS THE MOST ROMANTIC THING EVER!

And then Toby appeared, hanging out of the window of his room shouting . . .

And yeh, that killed the vibe dead, and Daniel said he had to go home.

Now I'm writing this, feeling distraught at the prospect of spending two weeks without him. It seems so unfair that as soon as we were reunited we were cruelly ripped apart again . . .

I said to Mum, 'It's just like the tragic love story of Romeo and Juliet!'

And she said, 'Yeh, exactly like that except they died and you are just going on a nice holiday for two weeks.'

God, why do parents have to be so irritating?!

8.15 p.m.

Fries Before Guys WhatsApp group:

> **ME:** Guess what?!?!?

> **POPPY:** OOH, fun game! Me first . . . You accidentally ate a bee?

ME: No. Something good.

JESS: You won 5 million pounds on the lottery?

ME: Less good than that.

POPPY: You went to the shop to buy a KitKat Chunky and it was Buy One, Get One Free?

ME: A bit better than that.

JESS: OMG, you kissed Daniel?!?!?

ME: Yes!!!!!!!!!

POPPY: OMG!!!!!!!

JESS: OMG!!!!!!!!!!!!!!!!!!

POPPY: How was it??? Did you slobber all over him?!

JESS: Did you use tongues?!

ME: No! I've told you – I'm never doing kissing with tongues. It looks gross! It was just a quick peck BUT it was on the lips. I don't know how to describe it really – I mean, no one let off any fireworks for us or anything, but it felt kind of . . . nice, I guess.

POPPY: That's so exciting, Lottie! So, are you boyfriend and girlfriend again?

ME: I don't know . . . we didn't say . . . I guess we'll see how it goes when I get back from holiday. 😎

JESS: SO exciting! Have a fab holiday, Lotts. xx

ME: Thanks, guys. xx

THOUGHT OF THE DAY:
My name is Lottie Rose Brooks. I am twelve years and nine months old, and today I had my very first kiss.

SUNDAY 7 AUGUST

7.15 a.m.

Got up at 3 a.m. because Dad booked us on the cheapest flight he could possibly find.

We are now sitting on the plane, and I feel like a zombie.

Bella is absolutely GAAAAAHHHHing her head off, Toby has his fart gun out, Dad's wearing a bucket hat because he thinks it makes him look 'down with the kids' and Mum's just asked if it's too early for a G&T.

The other passengers sitting all around us keep tutting and sighing. Honestly, it's so embarrassing!

Luckily, my seat is on the row in front of them so I'm basically pretending we are not related. When the flight attendant went past with her trolley and asked if there was anything I wanted, I said, '*Non merci, madame!*' in the hope that everyone would think I am an unaccompanied French exchange student.

To distract myself from the hullabaloo, I'm listening to
Harry Styles and daydreaming about the holiday . . .
eating croissants and pains au chocolat, using my
extensive knowledge of French, such as *bonjour*, *au revoir*
and *merci* . . . and erm . . . moving on . . . wearing my new
bikini in the pool! Lying on a sunbed with a towel over
my head so I can watch TikToks on my phone.

Ohh la la – it's going to be *très* good!

4.24 p.m.

We have just arrived at campsite **Le Petit Bois**,
which means 'the Little Wood'. It was a slightly stressful
journey. Mum said to Dad, 'Remember, they drive on the
opposite side of the road here,' just as Dad was about to
drive headlong into a massive lorry.

We are staying in a safari tent, which is big and beige
and has a nice wooden deck with sunbeds on it. Dad says
it's what's called 'glamping', which apparently means
glamorous camping, but I don't see what is glamorous
about having no toilet, shower or running water.

Our tent has four rooms – the living room/dining room/
kitchen and three bedrooms. Technically I'm not sure
they can be described as 'rooms' as I don't think pieces
of material count as 'walls'. However, that's just my
opinion.

Dad said, 'Right, first things first – beer!'

I said, 'WHOA! Hold on there, big fella. First things first –
what's the Wi-Fi password?'

He had the audacity to laugh!

'Lottie, we are camping – there is no Wi-Fi!'

'Sorry, Dad. I didn't quite catch that. What do you mean by *there is no Wi-Fi?*'

'I mean . . . there is no Wi-Fi. We are totally off-grid. Isn't it fabulous?'

At this point, dear reader, I began to hyperventilate. I started feeling sick and weak and I had to go and sit down and do some breathing exercises.

'So let me get this right – you have dragged me ALL the way to France, away from **ALL** my friends, and I won't even be able to use my phone?! Do you not understand that having access to a stable Wi-Fi connection is a basic human right?!'

'Oh, don't be dramatic, Lottie!'

'I'm not being dramatic. What on earth do you expect me to do here with no internet?!'

'There is LOADS to do. Why don't you go and explore while we finish unpacking?'

My response to that was **'URGH'** and an eyeroll so big that it made my eyeballs ache. Thanks, Dad!

Now I'm in my 'room' writing this and I can hear him muttering to Mum about me. 'If she's got an attitude like this already, Laura, imagine what she'll be like at fifteen. God help us!'

'I CAN HEAR YOU!' I shouted.

I don't think they understand that if I can't message Daniel for two weeks I will probably die. I mean, we've just had our first kiss FGS – it's a pretty monumental moment in a young girl's life!

Right – I'm going to check the campsite out. BRB.

6.12 p.m.

Just back from my explore. Apart from the lack of Wi-Fi, it's pretty cool here actually. (Don't tell Dad!) Well, much cooler than Sunny Beach in Wales anyway (which isn't particularly hard). I've drawn you a handy map to help you get your bearings. I've put the names in French because it may be useful if your French teacher suddenly springs a pop quiz on you (don't worry – you can thank me later).

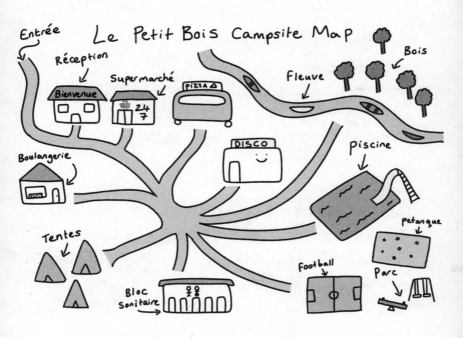

The good news is that Mum ordered takeaway pizza from the pizza van for dinner and it's just arrived – yum!

The pizza was SO good. It must be extra delicious here because France invented pizza . . . Hang on, maybe that was Italy?! What did France invent then? Oh . . . French fries, of course – doh!

Did England ever invent anything nice to eat?

Hmmmmm . . .

AHA, I've got it – the humble, yet incredibly delicious Pot Noodle.

I actually have six of the Chicken and Mushroom variety and six of the Beef and Tomato variety under my camp bed. I brought them in case there was nothing I could eat here. Not just a pretty face, eh?

I had forgotten that France invented fries though, so I should be fine anyway.

Gah, I'm rambling again. What I came here to tell you was that we've just met our neighbours in the tent next

door. They are called ... and I kid you not ... the Nutters!
Yep, I swear on my life! Cross my heart and hope to die.
(Incidentally that's a strange phrase, isn't it? Why would
anyone hope to die?!)

Here is a portrait of them ...

They seem quite nice and friendly. They've invited us
over to join them for a beer/Orangina. Dad is delighted
and keeps saying stuff like, 'You see, this is the beauty
of camping! Meeting other like-minded, outdoorsy
families!'

I don't know why he's described himself as 'outdoorsy', as he barely leaves the house except to go to work. Unless you count the local pub garden . . . which he probably does.

8.13 p.m.

Escaped back to the tent for a bit of peace. I have changed my opinion on the Nutters. Dad and Mum have struck up a good friendship with them (mostly revolving round the consumption of alcohol) but I'm a lot less keen.

The twins are nine years old and a bit intense. Hailey kept wanting to brush and plait my hair and Bailey kept staring at me and asking if I have a boyfriend – he's like nine, so how is that even relevant to him?!

The weirdest thing is that the entire family is obsessed with Kylie Minogue. They play her songs on a loop and seem to know every single word to every single song she's EVER written. Bonkers.

9.03 p.m.

Discovered that the tent doesn't offer much privacy –

Bella's stinky nappy smell has infiltrated my entire 'room' and Toby keeps undoing the zips and poking his head through the 'wall' and going **'SURPRISE!'** every twelve seconds, which is not irritating AT ALL.

Suddenly missing home and Jess, Poppy, Daniel and my hammies very much.

9.35 p.m.

I wonder if Daniel thought I was good at kissing? I wonder what he'd rate me out of ten? I'd rate him 8.5/10. I'm deducting 1 point because his lips were ever so slightly dry and maybe he should use some lip balm . . . The other 0.5 deduction is because of the BBQ Beef Hula Hoops taste . . . although TBH I didn't mind it that much. At least it wasn't Wotsits.

10.14 p.m.

Shattered but can't sleep.

Dad and Gary are singing 'I'm Spinning Around'. Badly. VERY BADLY.

Thank goodness – someone has finally called campsite security on them. (I strongly suspect it was Mum.) The security guard came over and gave them a lecture about respecting fellow campers. Apparently there is a 'no amplified music' rule after 10 p.m. Dad was quite cross because the music wasn't amplified so didn't break any rules. The security guy said that shouting counts too. Dad said it wasn't shouting, it was just singing, but they obviously agreed to disagree as he came home and got into bed, muttering to himself.

MONDAY 8 AUGUST

So tired. Barely slept. Bella was up screaming all night.
Toby woke up for a wee every twenty-five seconds, and
don't even get me started on Dad's snoring! Blimey,
he sounds like a brachiosaurus (not that I've heard a
brachiosaurus snoring, but I imagine it'd be loud like Dad).

I'm feeling anxious, weak and jittery. I think it's partly due
to tiredness but mostly due to withdrawal symptoms from
lack of internet access because I just worked out that I
haven't been online for an **ENTIRE TWENTY-FOUR HOURS**!!

If I knew who to complain to about this, I'd be writing
them a very strongly worded letter. I mean, why do places
with no Wi-Fi even exist?!

7.11 a.m.

Mum found me curled up in a ball, shaking. She took my
temperature and was being pretty sympathetic until I told

her I wasn't *exactly* feeling poorly *per se*.

I'm Scared without my phone.

Dad said that the fact that I am finding it so hard to cope without the internet only serves to prove that going off-grid will be a really good thing for me.

GOOD?! HOW?!??! He's so out of touch it's unbelievable!

8.17 a.m.

Mum managed to unroll me from my ball and I agreed to help her get breakfast. As soon as we stepped out of the tent on to the porch, we were immediately greeted by the Nutters!

'MORNING, CAMPERS! ENJOY THE LIE-IN, DID WE?!?'
shouted Gary.

I mean, what planet is he on?! It was like 7.30 a.m. so
hardly a lie-in. Apparently the Nutters get up every day
at 6 a.m. and then sit there waiting for the rest of the
campsite to wake up because 'who wants to waste a
second of camping fun times?'!

Er, me! I do.

They are v v odd.

Me and Mum went to the boulangerie and you'll be
proud to hear this, because I actually ordered breakfast
for everyone all by myself. I said, '*Deux croissants et trois
pains au chocolat, s'il vous plaît.*' And it worked. They totally
understood me. I paid with euros and I felt like a proper
French person.

When we got back, the Nutters were all sitting outside
their tent, in a line, still just staring at us.

Ate breakfast and Dad went off on a massive rant . . .

'Going off-grid will be really great for us as a family
because we can all be at one with nature and enjoy
seeing things with our eyes for what they are instead of
social-media content. We'll be able to properly connect
with each other and have meaningful conversations and
enjoy the simple things in life like . . . going on walks . . .
and hiking . . . and fishing . . . and going on nice walks . . .
and . . . things like that.'

'Dad, you've basically said walking three times, because
hiking is a type of walking, and you don't even like
fishing because that one time you caught a fish it bit you
when you took it off the hook and you were so scared
you threw it at Uncle Freddie and fell in the river!'

'I'm willing to give it another go!' he said crossly.

10.34 a.m.

OMG. He's STILL rabbiting on! If he says 'off-grid' one

more time I might have to kill him with the remaining croissants.

The twins just ran over and started circling me, going:
'WHAT ARE YOU DOING TODAY, LOTTIE?!? CAN WE COME WITH YOU, PLEEEEEASE, PLEEEEEASE?'

Then Hailey started grabbing at my hair and trying to plait it again and Bailey started doing more weird staring.

To get them off my back, I told them we were going to the pool and we *might* see them there. They immediately ran off to get their stuff ready. I fear I may have made a big mistake.

11.15 a.m.

OH MY GOD!

Something bad has happened! Like REALLY, REALLY bad!

I DO NOT HAVE MY NEW BIKINI!!!!!!!!

I must have been so distracted, thinking about Daniel and Pot Noodles, that I forgot to put it in my suitcase.

Worse still, I forgot to pack any of my other swimwear, so I have literally nothing to go swimming in AT ALL.

My options were this:

    1. Don't go swimming for the entire holiday (bad).

2. Borrow some of Mum's swimwear (also bad).

It's baking out here and I'm desperate to get into the pool so I've no choice but to go for option 2. The main problem with that is, erm, well . . . How do I say this? Mum's cup size is *significantly* larger than mine!

I feel like Toby demonstrated this pretty well . . .

Look, I can wear the booby bits as a hat!

2.25 p.m.

Well, I may have been wearing the unflattering baggy bikini of a forty-something-year-old woman (with the straps done up and double-knotted as tight as possible) but the good news is that the pool was really lovely and I found a great lounger right in the sun. I wanted to work on my tan so I could go back to school looking like a bronzed LA goddess and everyone would be, like, *Whoa, who is that?*

Unfortunately, Toby had other ideas and kept begging me to play Sharks. In case you aren't familiar with the game Sharks, it basically involves one person pretending to be a shark and then chasing the other person until they get them, then you pretend to eat them. Then the game starts again but the roles are swapped round with the shark becoming the person and vice versa. And so on . . . for eternity. It's pretty thrilling.

When you are bored of Sharks you can also move on to a game called Crocs, which is exactly the same as Sharks except instead of being a shark the chaser is a croc.

I'm even boring myself now. Sorry.

It got EVEN worse because the Nutter twins turned up. When I said earlier that it was a big mistake telling the twins we were going to *la piscine*, I should have said BIG mistake, like **MASSIVE**!!!!!!

They wanted to join in our game, but they decided to change it into a game called Shark Kiss Chase, where instead of getting eaten by the shark you got kissed. I really didn't want to be playing kiss chase with a couple of nine-year-olds. Also, I REALLY didn't want to be playing a game of kiss chase with my own brother. BLURGH.

Toby was just as horrified as me. He thinks girls stink and said he'd have to be paid one thousand million pounds to kiss one. (I'm sure you could barter him down a bit on that one though – it is A LOT of money!)

So we hatched a plan and told them we were going to the loo and then we hid behind the toilet block for twenty minutes until they got bored and left.

Now I'm back on my excellent sunlounger and writing this. I came up with a really clever game to play with Toby called **OLYMPIC DIVING CHAMPION**, which basically involves me pretending to watch him dive and shouting out scores out of ten.

I nearly got rumbled when I accidentally gave him a 9.5 for a belly flop but I just said that I got something stuck in my eye and everything was a bit blurry.

(3.25 p.m.)

I'm lying here looking at the beautiful pool and the bright blue sky, trying to appreciate them with the simplicity of humble off-grid eyeballs. But all I can think about is how this would make really good Instagram content.

I mean, is there any point even going away on holiday if you can't post about it on social media?!

OMG, Dad's just taken off his shorts to go for a swim
and he's wearing Speedos! He says that apparently
they prefer men to wear Speedos in France as it's more
hygienic.

Well, I personally prefer not to see my father in tiny
swimming knickers!

The most embarrassing dad on the entire planet!!!

Going to have to drag my sunbed round to the other side
of the pool now.

4.34 p.m.

Back at the tent. Thirty-two hours without Wi-Fi. I'm feeling nauseous, my head is pounding, and I have sweatier armpits than usual. That may be because I forgot to put deodorant on though.

4.44 p.m.

Have applied some more deodorant, which has helped with the sweaty-armpit problem but now my thumbs are seizing up. They are used to typing approx. 500 WhatsApp messages a day and now that's gone down to zero they don't know what to do with themselves. They'll probably fall off soon and then Mum and Dad will be sorry!

People will say to my parents, 'Oh no! What happened to your poor daughter's thumbs?' and they'll have to say, 'We heartlessly took her on an off-grid camping holiday in France.'

To try and keep my thumbs attached, I decided to exercise them by writing a postcard to Jess. Apparently sending postcards was very popular in the olden days. Mum laughed and said they often didn't arrive until after you were back home from holiday anyway – I mean, how utterly pointless is that?! Sometimes it blows my mind to think about how people used to survive without smartphones.

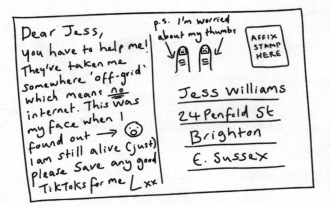

Dear Jess,
you have to help me!
They've taken me
somewhere 'off-grid'
which means no
internet. This was
my face when I
found out → ☺
I am still alive (just)
Please save any good
TikToks for me L xx

p.s. I'm worried
about my thumbs

AFFIX
STAMP
HERE

Jess Williams
24 Penfold St
Brighton
E. Sussex

6.03 p.m.

This is ridiculous. What if Jess needs to urgently contact me about the hammies? What if Daniel has messaged and he thinks I'm not replying because I don't like him? What if there is a new trend on TikTok and I don't know anything about it?!

Right, that's it. It's impossible to live like this. The off-grid lifestyle just isn't for me – I'm not a blimmin' cave person!

I'm going to find some Wi-Fi and I'm not coming back without it – wish me luck!

Decided that asking at reception was my best bet.

Went in and said, *'Je* want *le* Wi-Fi, *s'il vous plaît.'*

Luckily, the lady in there spoke English – she said she gets lots of teenagers coming in on their first day, clutching their phones and looking desperate. She also gave me the best news ever! You can get on the campsite Wi-Fi in the plaza area. She said the signal isn't great but it's strongest on the left side of the supermarché – apparently it's fondly known as the Wi-Fi Wall.

I went to investigate and to be honest it wasn't that hard to find . . .

Immediately checked my socials and messages, and the relief was instantaneous!

WhatsApp convo with Daniel:

DANIEL: Hey, Lottie, how's the holiday going?

ME: Sorry for the slow reply. It's been horrendous. I've only just managed to get online! It's going OK – Apart from my dad almost getting us evicted by a security guard for singing Kylie Minogue at the top of his lungs and the strange nine-year-old twins living in the tent next door who are borderline stalking me. Oh, and my thumbs are nearly falling off. How are you?

DANIEL: HA! 😂 How do you always get yourself into such mad situations?!

ME: I don't know – I blame my family. I think we are cursed or something. How are things with you?

DANIEL: Yeh, OK – but it's raining (as usual) and I'm pretty bored. Looking forward to seeing you when you get back!

ME: Looking forward to seeing you too! X

OMG OMG OMG!!!!!!!!!! I wonder if we'll finally get to go on our pier date, go on the ghost train and eat candyfloss in the sun!

I forced myself to calm down because next I needed to FaceTime Jess and check in on my hammies. Luckily, they look like they are having a fabulous time – phew!

PS I warned her that if she gets an overly dramatic postcard with some strange sad thumbs on, she should just throw it straight in the bin.

TUESDAY 9 AUGUST

Mum and Dad said, 'What do you fancy doing today?'

I wanted to say 'hang out by the Wi-Fi Wall' but I didn't think that would go down too well so I just said I didn't mind.

1.35 p.m.

Went and did a big shop in the French hypermarché (basically like a **MEGA** supermarket) and it was epic!

There are about 237 different varieties of Milka, LOADS of different types of Kinder chocolate I'd never heard of before and a million varieties of cereal. They also have these yummy Petit Ecolier biscuits, which have the thickest chocolate on top. Mum says she remembers having them when she went on a camping holiday to France when she was my age – they are très delicious!

My parents are usually much meaner when it comes to buying us nice snacks, but today they let us load the trolley up! I can only assume it was because they felt embarrassed about how much wine and beer they were buying.

Let's just get it in the car quickly!

Dad and Gary each gave me ten euros to take Hailey, Bailey and Toby to the kids' disco.

I could see the desperation in their eyes, so I managed to haggle them up from five.

It was as très uncool as suspected, but you'll never guess who was there doing the hokey-cokey . . .

Only Pete the Penguin, the mascot we met at Sunny Beach caravan park in Wales last year!

He nearly jumped out of his skin when I tapped him on the shoulder and he saw me standing there, but we had a big hug and it was so good to see a familiar face so many miles away from home.

I asked him how he's made it all the way here from Wales and he said he flew and then started laughing like a crazy person. Considering he is a penguin, you would think he would know that they can't actually fly!

He was busy fulfilling his entertainment-team duties, so we couldn't really chat much more, but I went to find him afterwards and guess where he was . . . hiding behind the launderette smoking! He had promised to try and give up last time I saw him, so I was bitterly disappointed.

He introduced me to his mate Geraldine the Giraffe, who

runs the kids' club – also a smoker, tsk tsk.

At least they had the decency to look ashamed of themselves.

8.35 p.m.

Daniel messaged me a reel of doggos dancing to the 'Chicken Wing, Chicken Wing, Hot Dog and Baloney' song and it was so funny I nearly weed my pants. Sorry if that's TMI.

I just like him SO much and we are so in tune with each other!

It made me miss him **V V MUCH**!

So I've made a calendar to count down the days until we are back together . . .

Mum saw it and said, 'Lottie, love . . . this is meant to be a lovely family holiday. It's a shame that you seem so eager to get home.'

I said, 'It's nothing personal, Mum – I just miss Daniel, that's all.'

'I know, but remember: you're only twelve. In a couple of

weeks you'll probably get a crush on somebody else, and you'll have forgotten all about him.'

'FYI, Mother, I'm nearly thirteen and I won't forget about him – I'm not that shallow! I've been wearing the necklace he bought me **EVERY** day and I'm **NEVER** going to take it off. This is more than just a crush . . . Maybe you've forgotten what it's like to be young and in love . . .'

'*Au contraire*. I'm not that old and I love your father very much!'

'Really?! Even when he's wearing his Speedos?'

'Well . . . maybe not quite so much then . . . but yes, even then. Look, there's a teenage disco tonight – why don't you go? You might meet someone your own age to hang out with. It could be fun.'

I said, 'OMG, I wouldn't be seen dead there. It'll just be full of losers!'

Lying in bed listening to my parents and the Nutters

swapping stories of 'crazy things' they did in their youth.
Judging by the content and bad language they are using,
I assume they think I'm asleep.

Dad just told a story of a time when he lost a bet and
had to run down the high street naked with a traffic cone
on his head. Apparently he got cautioned for indecent
exposure and had to spend the night in a cell!

(11.47 p.m.)

Can't get that horrific image of Dad out of my head.
Never going to be able to sleep now!

WEDNESDAY 10 AUGUST

Woken up at 7.07 a.m. by the twins who were leaning over me and breathing in my face. I almost had a heart attack.

I screamed at them because I was terrified – I mean, who even let them in?!??! Apparently no one – they just walked in. Would you believe it?!

Then Mum came into my room and said, 'Well, that wasn't very friendly, Lottie.'

I said, 'Well, would you like to be woken up by strange stalker twins breathing in your face?'

She couldn't really disagree with that TBF.

4.08 p.m.

We decided to go kayaking in the Ardèche for the day so we got dressed and started loading up the car. As we were leaving, Gary Nutter calls out, 'Looks like you guys are off on a fun day out. Where are you going?'

And Dad replied with, 'We're going kayaking in the Ardèche. See you when we get back!'

Can you guess what happened next . . .

They only went and followed us there!

I was actually having a pretty decent time until they arrived – which is rare with my family. I was in a kayak on my own and Dad was with Toby. Mum and Bella were watching from the beach, as apparently Bella is too young to hold a paddle properly.

I was cruising along, enjoying the lovely scenery, and then all of a sudden we turn round and there they are, right behind us.

I don't think I've ever paddled so hard before, just trying to get away from them. I guess at least my arms have had a good workout.

Someone seriously needs to teach those kids some boundaries! They are quite possibly the most annoying people I have ever met, and that's saying something, considering I have Toby as a brother.

How on earth are we going to cope with spending nine more days living next door to them?

OOH – there's finally something interesting to tell you!

I had gone to the Wi-Fi Wall to message Daniel, and I saw a boy standing there, chatting on his phone.

He was not just any boy – he was the most handsome boy I have EVER seen!

Yes, yes, I know I said that about Theo . . . and yes, also Daniel too . . . but, trust me, this boy was **EVEN HANDSOMER**!

He had lovely spiky jet-black hair, blue eyes and an amazing tan! I could not help but stare. Then he started speaking and OMG his accent was to die for!

When I got back to the tent, Mum asked me how Daniel was, and I realized that I had completely forgotten to message him. Just four days ago we had our very first kiss and then I see a handsome French boy and my brain feels like spaghetti – what is going on?!

THOUGHT OF THE DAY:
Maybe I am just a fickle, shallow twelve-year-old after all!

THURSDAY 11 AUGUST

11.45 a.m.

Keep thinking about Handsome French Boy (HFB).

Since meeting him, my swimwear situation has suddenly felt much more serious, so I begged Mum and Dad to drive me to a shopping centre to find something more age-appropriate and less humongous around the bust.

They were just about to relent when Toby appeared from his 'bedroom' waving my new bikini over his head going, 'Ha ha, tricked you!'

Like, in what world is that even vaguely funny?! I swear I would have killed him had I not been so overjoyed to get it back.

1.49 p.m.

Walked around the campsite looking for the HFB but no luck. Had nothing else to do so I went to the supermarché to look for things to spend my twenty euros on.

Found the best thing ever! A massive inflatable flamingo! It has a cup holder and everything.

Going to take it down to the pool later and float about on it. Hopefully HFB will be there and be impressed by how amazingly cool I look.

3.46 p.m.

I looked proper cool on my flamingo but there is no HFB at the pool – where is he?!?!??!

4.56 p.m.

Made the mistake of letting my little sister have a go on the flamingo and she wouldn't get off it. Every time Mum tried to pick her up, she went absolutely crazy. I really wouldn't have minded but I was desperate to get a good photo for Instagram and in the end I had no choice but to have Bella in the shot too.

I was worried she was seriously cramping my style but when I uploaded the pic I got the most likes **EVER**. So maybe it was actually me cramping Bella's style?!?!

67 likes
Cruisin with little Sis! ☺
Good times and tan lines
Girls just wanna have sun

7.07 p.m.

A random guy called out 'Hey, Lottie!' to me. He was standing with a lady who I also didn't know so I was like **EH?!**

I must have looked very confused as the guy then goes, 'It's me – Martin!'

'Sorry, I think you have me confused with somebody else,' I said.

'No, I don't . . . I'm Pete the Penguin – my real name is Martin, remember? And this is Sarah, AKA Geraldine the Giraffe.'

'**OMG, NO, NO!** Go away! I mean, hi . . . but I don't want to see you as people – it's too weird!'

Then I put my hands over my eyes and ran in the opposite direction. I hope they didn't think I was too rude, but thinking of them being normal human beings is just way too upsetting. And yes I do realize that makes me sound about four years old.

(11.01 p.m.)

Another raucous night at la tente Brooks et la tente Nutters.

They are now on first-name terms with the campsite security guard who comes by every night to tell them to shut up. Even I know quite a lot about Philippe. He's sixty-one, divorced with two kids, still loves his ex-wife and hates Kylie Minogue.

Tonight Dad is doing impressions of famous people (who are obviously so old that I've never heard of any of them). They all sound the same and no one is able to guess who he is meant to be. He keeps going, 'Oh, I know, I know . . . you'll definitely get this one!'

But no one ever gets it.

I wish he'd give up – he's just embarrassing himself.

FRIDAY 12 AUGUST

Woke up and went to the Wi-Fi Wall. Jess had sent
me a picture of the hammies. She's teaching them to
play tennis and has made them little rackets out of
toothpicks and string! They aren't doing too well just yet,
but it's the thought that counts.

I also saw Pete there (thankfully in his penguin onesie).
Apparently even campsite employees aren't treated to a
proper broadband connection – unbelievable!

He looked a bit sad, so I said, 'Are you OK, Pete? You seem
a bit down.'

He sighed. 'I'm twenty-seven years old, Lottie, and I'm a mascot in a crappy campsite in the South of France! It's just not the sort of life I imagined myself living.'

'It's better than Wales though, right?' I said.

He smiled. 'Yes, it's better than Wales, but I don't have anything to show for myself. I live in a tent, I have to stand against a wall to get Wi-Fi, and I don't even have a girlfriend.'

'Is there anyone you . . . like?'

'Well . . . I mean . . . don't tell anyone this . . . but I do actually like Sarah.'

'Who's Sarah?'

'Sorry, sorry. I mean, I like Geraldine the Giraffe.'

'Oh, wow, really? That's amazing! Why don't you ask her out?'

'Well, believe it or not, Lottie, I'm actually a pretty shy guy.'

'I think you mean you are a pretty shy penguin!'

'Yes, sorry. I wish I had the confidence to just go for it, you know?'

'I totally get you, Pete, and don't worry – maybe I can help. I'll try and come up with a plan!'

Exciting – now I have a matchmaking mission!

SATURDAY 13 AUGUST

OMG, I found HFB!

I was walking back from the dishwashing area where my parents had cruelly forced me to wash up the lunch stuff and then all of a sudden there he was, just standing in front of me. I must have been so dazzled by his beauty that I dropped the washing-up bowl on the floor and all the cutlery and plates fell out.

HFB ran towards me and said . . .

He sounded dreamy and I felt my heart begin to melt. Suddenly I wished I had paid more attention in French lessons.

HFB started to help me pick up the dishes and put them back in the washing-up bowl, which was very kind of him. I racked my brain for something to say. What was 'thank you' in French again??!?! Oh yes . . .

'*Merci!*' I said proudly.

The boy smiled, clearly impressed that I could in fact speak his language.

'*Comment tu t'appelles?*' he asked.

I knew this one too!!!!!

'*Je m'appelle Lottie.*'

My God, I was practically fluent!

'*Ahh, Lottie. Je m'appelle Antoine.*'

OMG!!!!!!!!!!!!

The same as my mango!!!!!!!

Was this fate?!

I thought about telling him that I had a mango called
Antoine with googly eyes that I used to practise kissing
on before my mum blended it into a smoothie and drank
it, but that would have been above my capabilities and
also . . . it sounded kinda weird.

Instead I said, 'Ahh Antoine, nicey *nom*! Erm . . . *quel âge
as-tu?*'

'*J'ai douze ans, et toi?*

'*Douze ans*, also!'

OMG – we were also the exact same age. This was getting
spooky!

By this point I had used up practically all my French, so
we did lots of laughing about nothing, which was great

and then he helped me carry the washing-up back to the
tent. I desperately wanted to say something cool/funny
before he left. Come on, Lottie – think . . . AHA.

'*J'aime le fromage.*'

In case you don't speak French, that means 'I love
cheese' and I do!

Antoine replied, '*Moi aussi. J'aime le fromage.*'

I assumed that meant he loves cheese too and thus we
are a match made in cheesy heaven!

Then he said, '*Au revoir,*' and turned and left.

Now I'm lying on my camp bed dreaming of this
handsome, cheese-loving stranger and hoping our paths
will cross again.

7.25 p.m.

At the Wall of Wi-Fi.

Fries Before Guys WhatsApp group:

ME: Met a HFB!!

JESS: A Highly Flammable Baboon?

ME: No!

POPPY: A Hungry Funky Bunny?

ME: What?! No! A Handsome French Boy!

POPPY: OOOOH, TELL US MORE!!!

ME: He's called Antoine and he's sooooooo cute!

JESS: Is he a mango?

ME: NO! He's an actual human. But I can't help but think that Antoine the mango was a prophecy or something and this was meant to be . . .

POPPY: So, what's he like? Did you talk to him?

ME: Yes, we spoke in French. Madame Dubois would have been so proud!

JESS: *Lottie, tu es si sophistiquée!*

ME: What?!

JESS: Never mind. So, are you seeing him again!?

POPPY: Yeh, come on – we want details. Did you kiss him???

ME: NO! I've only known him for like ten minutes.

POPPY: Would you like to though?!?!

ME: EEK, I dunno!

JESS: But what about Daniel?

ME: Daniel?!

POPPY: Errr, the guy you've been dating?! The one you had your first kiss with a week ago?!?

ME: Oh yeh. Um. Oops. I kind of keep . . . forgetting about him.

JESS: I smell trouble. 😊

POPPY: Poor Daniel. 🥲

Argh, I feel really guilty now, especially as I remembered I never replied to Daniel's message from the other day, so I sent him a quick reply saying I was fine and that I'd see him soon. I looked down at the necklace that he'd bought me.

what Sort of terrible person am I ?!

THOUGHT OF THE DAY:
I'm about as shallow as a really
shallow puddle that is so shallow it
is barely even a puddle any more and
more like a slightly-wet-looking bit of
pavement.

SUNDAY 14 AUGUST

(10.32 a.m.)

Woke up late. Must have been tired from Bella's all-night milk-guzzling **PARTAAAAY** because everyone was sitting at the table outside eating croissants and drinking juice and coffee.

'Ahhh, she finally awakes!' said Dad, picking up something from the table. 'Here . . . your French friend dropped this off this morning.'

It was an envelope with 'Lottie' written on the front. I didn't want to read it in front of them, so I took it back into the tent and tore it open excitedly.

Chère Lottie,

First one first – forgive my bad time of English, I ask my brother, Hugo, to help me translate. I hope he is making good jobs of it.

It was fantastical to meet your fine person on the day before today. Never had I been so glad to pick up a plate of the plastic variety.

I'm shocked to believe that we both are twelve and have a love of cheese – très fantastique! I'm sure we have many more coincidences between us, not discovered until later.

Would you like to take a nature walk with me tomorrow for more chatty chat?

If the answer would be yes, I will see by the toilet block at 2 p.m.

Love of Antoine x

PS My brother is much better-looking than me and I have a fungal infection that makes my feet smell like rotting fish.

OMG!!!!!!!!!!!! He's written me a love letter!

Well, sort of anyway. The main thing is he likes me, he likes cheese, and I am meeting an HFB at the toilet block tomorrow for a chatty chat! *C'est très romantique!*

10.37 a.m.

I really hope that the rotting fishy feet was a joke though!

4.45 p.m.

I've been so happy today that I've barely felt annoyed with anyone. I played Sharks in the pool with Toby and the twins for ages (I drew the line at Shark Kiss Chase though), and then I let Hailey plait my hair for about an hour and a half and I didn't even complain when Bailey kept repeatedly asking to be my boyfriend.

7.45 p.m.

Daniel messaged back to see if we could FaceTime but I've been so busy thinking about Antoine and our toilet-block date that I've not had time to reply – again! Mum was right about everything – poor, poor Daniel!

But whatever. I have more pressing issues on my mind, like what to wear tomorrow to impress Antoine with a Parisian-chic look. We are nowhere near Paris, but you get what I mean. It's a shame I didn't put much thought into my packing. If I'd have known I was going to meet an HFB, I wouldn't have filled the majority of my suitcase with Pot Noodles.

8.12 p.m.

Good God. It's all kicked off. Apparently earlier when I was daydreaming about Antoine I accidentally by mistake said 'yes' when Bailey asked if he could be my boyfriend.

Now he's told **EVERYONE**, and Nana Nutter just came over and asked when we were getting married.

I've tried to explain that it was a simple clerical error on my part, but Bailey keeps shouting, 'BUT LOTTIE, YOU PINKY PROMISED!'

We've negotiated an agreement. I will be Bailey's 'girlfriend' for twenty-four hours **ONLY**, I will allow **ONE** photo of us together (he wants to show it to his mates) and there will be absolutely **NO** physical contact whatsoever. (He wanted a kiss but there is zero chance I will be wasting my second-ever kiss on nine-year-old Bailey Nutter!!)

The Olds are at it again. They have placed a parasol pole over the back of two patio chairs and are limbo dancing under it (badly) while singing (also badly), 'How low can you go!'

Philippe has already been over twice to tell them to be quiet, but they keep trying to convince him to have a go at the limbo. I think he needs to get tougher with them, personally.

URGH. They started playing Snog Marry Avoid and I had had enough, so I went out myself and scolded them pretty badly. Hopefully that will be the last of it!

MONDAY 15 AUGUST

Once I had finally got to sleep, I ended up having a very cheesy dream. It started off really well – I met Antoine and we went for a walk, then stopped for the most delicious cheese sandwiches and cheesecake to eat. **YUM!** Then we went to a beautiful forest. I looked up at the trees and noticed that they were growing various cheese products like Babybel, Dairylea and Cheestrings. We picked some and ate some more, then we got thirsty but had nothing to drink so we found a fresh spring and drank some of it but it was cheesy-flavoured spring water, which was actually pretty gross. Suddenly the weather turned bad and it started raining but the rain was made of cheese and then it rained so much we were washed away in a **BIG RIVER OF CHEESE**. I managed to get home but I absolutely stank of Camembert and Brie! Unfortunately, Antoine was declared missing and was never heard from again. Quite a sad ending really. I hope he didn't die. Although I guess drowning in cheese isn't the worst way to go.

Anyway, luckily that was all in my head and today I have a date!

9.14 a.m.

So cross at Bailey – I knew this would happen!!

Go on, just one kiss! A really tiny one!

NO WAY!! WE HAD A DEAL!!

10.56 a.m.

Oh, for goodness' sake! Mum is unhappy about me going off to meet a boy at the toilet block – so overprotective!

'Look, put it this way, Lottie, if you had a twelve-year-old daughter and she was proposing to go and meet a

complete stranger in a foreign country, would you be
happy for her to go?'

I said, 'Yes, of course I would!' (However, I guess I could
see her point.)

So, the upshot is she's coming with me to check that
he isn't a psychopath, then she promised if everything
seemed fine, she would leave us alone for our chatty-
chat nature walk.

(4.23 p.m.)

I'm in **LOVE**!!!!!!!!!

Right, so it all went REALLY well. Well, apart from one bit
(which I'll get to later).

Mum came and said '*Bonjour*' to Antoine, then he pointed
to a tent near the toilet block and said, '*Ma famille.*' We
all went over, and Mum waved and they waved back
and there was lots of nervous laughter and Mum said,
'*Bonjour la fam of Antoine, me la fam de la Lottie. Lottie et
Antoine jolie walk, non?*'

God knows what she was on about. They just laughed at her and said 'Oui!' Then luckily everyone seemed satisfied that we were just two normal kids going on a normal walk and not a pair of criminals, so Mum said that we could go off on our own as long as we stayed inside the campsite and we were back in one hour.

The date itself was great. In some ways it actually helped that neither of us could speak the other one's language much, as we had to accept early on that there would be long silences . . . and it meant I had to speak less, which was good because we all know my track record of coming out with really random weird things in front of boys I like.

We basically went around the campsite and talked about things we liked, mostly because that's all we knew how to say. I used my French and he used his English so it was educational for us both.

ME:	*J'aime les croissants.*
ANTOINE:	I like chocolate.
ME:	*J'aime les belles fleurs.*
ANTOINE:	I like a big tree.
ME:	*J'aime les chiens.*

ANTOINE:	I like kittens.
ME:	*J'aime les frites.*
ANTOINE:	I like chips also.
ME:	*J'aime le steak de bœuf.*
ANTOINE:	I like roost beef!

We laughed at that one! I think he was making a joke.
I couldn't think of words for more things I liked so I
changed tactic.

ME:	*Je déteste les maths.*
ANTOINE:	I don't like broccoli.
ME:	*Je déteste le Donald Trump.*
ANTOINE:	Ahhh, I hate Donald Trump also!
ME:	WOW!

I couldn't believe how much we had in common – it was
simply incredible!

By that point I was running out of things I knew how to
say in French, and Mum would be expecting me back,
so I said, 'I have to go now, Antoine.' I didn't know how

to say that in French so I just said it in English but with a French accent. (Hopefully that made it easier to understand.)

He replied, '*Est-ce que je te verrai vendredi soir à la discothèque pour les ados?*'

I had no clue what he was talking about, but as we were by the Wi-Fi Wall I Google-Translated it on my phone and it turned out he was asking me to go to the teenage disco on Friday night!

'*Oui, Antoine! Oui!*'

'*Génial, Lottie!*'

And then the not-so-good bit . . .

Enter Bailey.

'Hey, get your hands off her – she's **MY GIRLFRIEND**!!' he shouts as he starts pummelling Antoine in the stomach.

Antoine looked super confused and I was horrified!

I don't think he knew what on earth I was talking about, and I was only making things worse trying to explain our bizarre relationship deal so I just said, '*Au revoir*,' and then manhandled Bailey back to the tent.

'How did it go?' asked Mum when we got there.

'**AMAZING!** He asked me to go to the teen disco!'

'I thought you wouldn't be seen dead at the teen disco because it was full of losers?'

'*Au contraire, ma mère!* That was before I knew it would be full of . . . Antoine.'

'Oh, I see . . . and what about Daniel? A few days ago you implied he was the love of your life . . .'

'Jeez, I'm only twelve, Mum – I can't be expected to know what I'm talking about, can I?!'

(**8.45 p.m.**)

Me and Bailey are officially over. He's crying and I'm celebrating by eating an entire packet of Petit Ecolier biscuits. *Vive la France!*

TUESDAY 16 AUGUST

Went to the beach today. I would have rather stayed at the campsite with my HFB but Mum and Dad were banging on about having a 'nice family day out' again. At least I managed to convince them that we should NOT INCLUDE the Nutters. (I don't think they quite understand how stressful it is to have a stalker.)

We had to sneak off when they weren't looking so that they didn't follow us. I asked Dad why we couldn't just be honest and tell them we wanted some alone time and he said it wasn't the way British people do things.

Bella absolutely loved the beach (sort of); she's never been on a sandy beach before because it's all stones in Brighton. I think Mum found it all quite exhausting though because this is what Bella did on loop:

1. Scream to be put down on the sand.

2. Grab fistfuls of sand and put it in her mouth.

3. Scream because she didn't like having sand in her mouth.

4. Scream while Mum tried to clean sand out of her mouth.

5. Go back to step 1 and repeat.

This went on and on and on until Mum reached breaking point. Bella was briefly distracted by a banana but then she dropped it in the sand and all hell broke loose. The entire beach went silent. It was mortifying. I had never heard her **GAAAAHHHH** so loud! Then she did an angry protest poo in her swimming nappy and Mum looked like she was about to burst into tears.

Meanwhile me and Toby decided to bury Dad in the sand, which was quite fun, especially when we gave him a massive pair of boobs and took loads of good photos. (Must remember to send them to Nan and Grandad when we get home.)

Then he fell asleep for about two hours and unfortunately he had forgotten to put sun cream on his bald head so, when he finally woke up, he was kinda burnt . . .

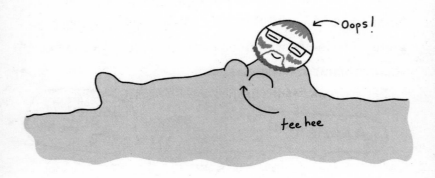

WEDNESDAY 17 AUGUST

9.03 a.m.

Oh dear. Dad woke up in a very bad mood – he looks like
a very angry, very red Humpty Dumpty.

10.02 a.m.

Just discovered I got my period – it caught me by
surprise because they still aren't regular yet. (I read in
my puberty book that apparently it can take a couple of
years for them to even out.)

I had a bit of a panic because we still have a few days of
holiday left and I wanted to go swimming.

Told Mum and she asked if I wanted to try using a
tampon. I was worried as I'd only used pads before, but
she said it's totally safe at my age *if* I felt comfortable
doing it.

I mean, I didn't at first. I looked at the instructions and

pictures and I freaked out. But Mum helped explain how they work so I'm about to give it a go. Wish me luck!

Winner, winner, chicken dinner! You'll be pleased to know Mission Tampon was a complete success.

Without going into details, it took a few goes to get it right, but once it was *ahem* 'in the right place' I couldn't even feel it.

(Kind of wish I hadn't shouted that across the whole toilet block TBH.)

Looks like Cinderlottie is off to the swimming pool after all!

(11.37 a.m.)

By the pool, hoping to bump into Antoine.

Bailey is harassing me to go out with him, and Hailey is chasing Toby round the pool asking for a kiss. I don't think I've ever seen him look so scared!

(12.34 p.m.)

Toby just pulled some tampons out of my bag and goes, **'HA HA – I'VE FOUND YOUR SWEETS! NOW YOU'VE GOT TO SHARE THEM!'**

I just thought I'd sit back and let him find out what they were the hard way . . .

How are you meant to eat it then?!

He ended up super confused so Mum took him to one side and gave him a fast-track introduction to periods and women's sanitary products. He looked like he was about to cry when she was finished explaining what tampons were actually used for – it was hilarious!

3.25 p.m.

Antoine eventually turned up. We had a swim (the tampon worked fine and didn't let me down – what a game changer!) and then I asked him if he was hungry by sort of rubbing my tummy and making an eating gesture. He said 'Oui!' so we walked back to our tent for lunch.

I wanted to showcase some of England's finest cuisine, so I made him a Pot Noodle.

So relieved he liked it, as it would have been a total deal-breaker for me.

8.24 p.m.

Just realized Daniel's necklace is missing! It must have come off in the pool earlier . . . I mean, I know it was probably only cheap, but he bought it for me to remember him by and now I feel really bad . . . both for losing it and, er, not doing a very good job of the 'remembering him' part.

THURSDAY 18 AUGUST

The campsite is hosting a talent show on Saturday night! Dad and Gary are very excited about it.

They are pairing up to do a Kylie Minogue tribute! I've tried my hardest to convince them not to, but they aren't having any of it.

Toby wanted to enter with a 'fart show' (I refused to even ask what that involves) but luckily it's over-eighteens only.

Pete the Penguin and Geraldine the Giraffe are the judges and there is a 100-euro prize. Everyone is very excited about it.

Except me.

As usual I will be hiding under a chair pretending I don't know any of them.

PS Looked for Daniel's necklace in the pool today but I couldn't find it. I hope he won't be upset with me. ☹

FRIDAY 19 AUGUST

5.24 p.m.

I've been spending the afternoon wondering what to wear tonight. I don't have anything at all disco-ish so I'm going to have to go dead casual, which I'm kind of relieved about as I never feel that comfortable when I get all dressed up anyway.

I decided on trainers, denim shorts and a black vest top. I haven't brought any make-up with me, but Mum let me borrow some of her mascara and perfume and I think I looked all right.

I'm nervous though. I really wish I had Jess and Poppy here to go with because I'll feel pretty self-conscious about walking in there on my own.

9.45 p.m.

So I arrived at the teen disco a bag of nerves. Bailey secretly followed me there and attempted to get in by speaking in a strange deep voice but unfortunately his height gave him away and Geraldine, who was working on the door, had to call his parents to come and collect him.

Part of me kind of wouldn't have minded Bailey coming in with me because I couldn't see Antoine anywhere and I felt super awkward. I went to the bar and ordered a lemonade, just for something to do. Because I was so nervous, I downed it really quickly and then I started feeling kinda drunk – sugar seems to have that effect on me.

Pete was DJing and he obviously saw me on my own because he announced over his mic: 'And this one goes out to the one and only Lottie Brooks!' and he started playing 'Stay' by Justin Bieber and The Kid LAROI.

I **LOVE** that song and when I hear music I like, my body takes over. So, it wasn't long before I was right in the middle of the dance floor using all my best moves.

Then suddenly from behind I felt a tap on my shoulder. It was Antoine. I'd been so absorbed in my dancing that

I hadn't seen him come in and I wondered how long he'd been watching. The good thing was that he didn't seem put off by it. In fact, he got on the floor and started breakdancing! It wasn't long before the entire disco was gathered round us, clapping and cheering.

TBH this was an easier date than the chatty-chat walk because we let our limbs communicate through the music and it was **SO MUCH FUN**! I made sure I got a selfie too as I was desperate to show him off to the girls.

OOH and as we were on the way out I whispered to Geraldine that I thought Pete liked her. I think she smiled and blushed but it was a bit hard to see her face properly under the massive costume.

Fries Before Guys WhatsApp group:

ME: So . . . this is Antoine! We've just been to a disco!

POPPY: OOOOOH, you are right – he is hot!

JESS: Poppy, watch out – you are objectifying him . . .

POPPY: Oops, sorry. I mean, he looks like he has a nice personality. 😊

JESS: Much better! Did you have a fun night, Lotts?

ME: Yeh, it was great. We did some pretty crazy dancing . . . but it made me miss you guys!

POPPY: Awww we miss you too. Can't wait to see you when you get back!

JESS: Don't forget it's my birthday on Monday! 🎉 🎉

ME: As if I would! Have you decided what to do yet?

JESS: Looks like it's going to be hot so how about going to the pier? My mum said she would get us unlimited passes for the rides?

ME: Woohoo! Sounds awesome!

POPPY: Can't wait. xxx

SATURDAY 20 AUGUST

This morning I crossed the last day off my makeshift calendar. I can't believe we are going home tomorrow!

I'm feeling kind of happy and sad . . . happy to be getting back to my hammies and my friends but sad because I hate to admit it to my parents but it has been a pretty excellent holiday.

I really don't know what I'll say to Daniel when I see him again . . . Isn't it weird how when you are on holiday you almost feel like you are living an entirely different life?

There is no point worrying about it now though. I'm determined to make the most of my last day with lots of swimming, sunbathing and chilling out. But it's going to be weird without Antoine because his family is leaving today – he's coming round in a minute to say goodbye (sob sob).

Antoine has gone! Hey, that rhymes (kinda).

He and Hugo came over to our tent early this morning . . .

'*Bonjour*, Lottie. I go home now. Sad time!' said Antoine.

'*Bonjour*, Antoine. *Oui*, I am sad time also,' I replied.

Then he started speaking in French and I couldn't understand a word of it.

I looked to Hugo for help.

'He says you look like a piece of organic asparagus.'

'Er . . . thanks, I guess. Can you tell him it was nice to meet him, and I'll miss him?'

Hugo and Antoine speak lots of French I don't understand

'He says he will miss you too, and he would like to cut one of his arms off and give it to you as a gift.'

'Tell him, wow, well, that's very generous, but I have enough of my own arms. Thank you though.'

More French chat

'He says, he understands about the arms, and maybe one day if you ever come back to France, he would love to show you his collection of boogers and belly-button fluff.'

'Tell him, I would like that very much.'

Then we all laughed a lot. It was probably one of the strangest conversations I've ever had but I enjoyed it anyway.

Before they left, we swapped email addresses and phone numbers and promised to keep in touch – I hope we do, as it would be sad if I never heard from him again.

Dad and Gary have been practising their Kylie tribute
act all day. I'm not going to lie – they sound terrible. The
worst part is that they are going to dress up in wigs and
gold hot pants. Apparently Gary always brings his gold
hot pants on holidays in case there is an opportunity
to perform as Kylie. Considering he has also brought
a spare pair, I assume this isn't the first time he's
convinced another random holidaymaker to join him!

We are at the talent show. Dad and Gary are backstage
waiting to go on . . . The quality of the acts so far is
pretty low. We've seen a juggler that couldn't juggle, a
magician who said they could guess the card, but, er
. . . didn't guess the right card, a gymnast who tried to
do the splits and then got stuck like that and had to be
carried offstage, and a guy who could quack like a duck.
(Relatively impressive as animal impressions go.)

I hate to say it, but I think Dad and Gary have actually
got a good shot at winning!

They are onstage and I'm watching from behind my
fingers! They have chosen to sing 'I Should Be So Lucky',
which is funny because I don't think anyone in the
audience feels very lucky having to watch two middle-
aged dads prance about the stage in teeny-tiny gold
hot pants.

If Kylie had to see this – I think she'd be appalled.

To be fair, they did get a lot of laughs though – so I think
it's between them and Duck Guy.

Oh, hang on. Late entry!! Nana Nutter has arrived with a hula hoop.

OMG – look at her go!

The crowd love her, and Gary is fuming! He and Dad thought they had it in the bag.

The wait for the results is super tense. Pete and Geraldine have been deliberating for over ten minutes. This is nail-biting stuff!

The results are in . . . **DRUM ROLL** . . .

Nana Nutter was crowned the champion  with her hula-hooping act – TBH she was brilliant and a well-deserving winner.

Duck Guy got second place and Dad and Gary got third.

They got awarded (plastic) medals but they refused to wear them, which was very unsportsmanlike. I told them it's the taking part that counts but they are being very sulky.

Gary is cross with Nana because she didn't even say she was entering, so he feels like she's gone behind his back. Apparently she also uses her 'poor mobility' to avoid making herself cups of tea – now he knows the truth, he says he is never making her another cup of tea ever again!

Nana Nutter spent her 100-euro winnings on beer, wine and Orangina in the supermarché so we can have a final-night party at our tents – **ALL IS FORGIVEN!**

Pete the Penguin and Geraldine the Giraffe are coming to the party . . . along with the juggler who can't juggle, the magician who is not very magic and Duck Guy. Oh, and their families too! The lady who did the splits said she'll pop along later if she can get her legs to work again.

9.35 p.m.

Everyone is drunk and dancing to Kylie – Gary looks like he's having the time of his life.

9.45 p.m.

Bailey has taken a shine to the Bad Juggler guy's daughter. I can't deny it is a HUGE relief. Meanwhile Hailey is playing kiss chase with Toby (again).

OMG Toby has had his first kiss! Not quite sure it was consensual though . . .

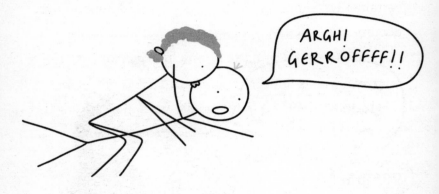

ARGH! GERROFFFF!!

10.05 p.m.

Philippe the security guard showed up and told everyone off for being too noisy. **AGAIN.** Then he realized that two thirds of the campsite were here so he decided to stay and join in the fun too.

10.26 p.m.

OOOOOH, Pete has asked Geraldine to dance!!!

ARGH!!!! Pete and Geraldine are kissing! Incidentally, have you ever seen a giraffe and a penguin kiss? It's certainly not something you see in a David Attenborough documentary . . .

Um, you do know that's not actually my mouth?!

10.49 p.m.

OMG – Nana Nutter is dancing with Philippe the security guard. Love is clearly in the air tonight.

URGH!! Nana and Philippe are doing proper French kissing with tongues – it looks even more disgusting IRL!! The rest of the Nutters are mortified. I just feel quite glad that for once someone else's family are being more embarrassing than mine.

Right, that's it. I'm going to bed. I'm putting my earplugs in and my eye mask on. I do not want to see or hear any more!

SUNDAY 21 AUGUST

Got up early and went out to survey the damage. I found Philippe asleep under the patio table!

I woke up Mum, Dad and the Nutters and made them get to work cleaning up the mess. Dad and Gary were still in their hot pants! I mean, honestly . . . you'd think I was the adult around here.

Nana Nutter was AWOL. Apparently all the hula-hooping last night had set off her arthritis. Personally, I think she was too embarrassed to face Philippe after their 'shenanigans' last night!

11.11 a.m.

We are just about to leave, and I feel pretty sad.

Pete and Geraldine came to wave us off. They make the cutest couple and I hope they invite me to their wedding!

It was quite emotional saying goodbye to the Nutters too. Nana finally dared to show her face and Philippe was absolutely delighted – they are quite sweet together really.

I can't believe I'm saying this after I was so desperate to get home, but I'm going to miss everyone. Deffo not Bailey though.

OK, OK . . . even Bailey (a really tiny bit).

11.29 a.m.

Changed my mind – I won't miss Bailey AT ALL!!!!

5.12 p.m.

Finally home!

It was a bit touch-and-go over whether we would be able to board the plane after Toby decided to inform the man at the check-in desk that he had a bomb in his bag. He found that incredibly funny. The rest of us, less so.

Opened my suitcase to unpack (still had three Pot Noodles left – result!) and I found a letter from Antoine. I guess he must have snuck it in before he left. The translations are a bit strange again. (I can't help but wonder if his older brother might be having a laugh at our expense? But never mind – it is still **SUPER CUTE** . . .)

> *Chère Lottie,*
>
> *It was so amazing meeting you on your holibobidays – you are fun and funny and you make me do frequent belly laughs, and sometimes you make me laugh so much that my bottom goes tooty toot!*

445

I like the way your hair looks like a horse's tail and your colour of eye is so blue it is like diving into a deep toilet bowl. I like the way you introduce me to the delicious hot-water noodles in a plastic pot, a fond experience for my tongue buds indeed! I also wanted to speak of your delighting smell, which is reminding me of cat food.

I will really miss you and will think of you all the time on all the days. Except Tuesday from 4–5 p.m. when I have my trombone lessons. It would make my eyeballs explode with happy if you would consider me to be a boyfriend of yourself?

Please write me back with a pencil in a timely manner,

Love of Antoine x

PS I was thinking of gifting you a kiss on your last night, but I was nerved you might find my face coming quickly at your face to be an unwelcome happening.

OMG I can't believe he was thinking about kissing me!
OMG I can't believe he wants to be my boyfriend! . . . Do I
smell like cat food though, as that's quite alarming?

7.26 p.m.

Jess has just left. She popped round with my hammies
and it was SO good to be reunited with them!

I showed Jess my letter from Antoine. She began reading
it and immediately started laughing, which I thought
was *slightly* rude.

'He thinks your eyes look like toilet water!' she read, giggling.

'Don't be mean! His English wasn't that good.'

'And that . . . and that you –' she was laughing so hard now she could barely speak – 'smell of cat food?!'

'Jess!'

'I'm sorry, Lottie, but he does sound a bit odd.'

'Yeh, well . . . you didn't meet him. He was SO good-looking!'

'Looks aren't everything though, right?'

'I know, but we also had lots in common.'

'Like what?'

'Loads of stuff . . . like . . . we both love cheese!'

'Oh, wow. Well, I'm glad you found the only other human on the planet who loves cheese!' she said, rolling her eyes.

'Don't be sarcastic!'

'Sorry. What about Daniel though? I know he's not an HFB but remember when you used to **REALLY** like him?'

I sighed. 'I know. And I do . . . It's just all pretty confusing.'

At this point she leant over and started sniffing me and I panicked that maybe I had bad BO or something. 'What are you doing, Jess?!'

'Sorry, but I think Antoine was right . . . you do smell of cat food!'

'OMG, Jess! I'm going to throw you out in a minute!!'

'Sorry!' she said, doubling over. 'But I'd better go soon anyway . . . You need to write Antoine back . . . *with a pencil . . . in a timely manner!*'

I'm not ashamed to say that I proceeded to whack her over the head with my pillow at this point.

7.57 p.m.

Maybe you can help . . . Would you be able to fill out this survey for me?

1.) WHO SHOULD LOTTIE GET TOGETHER WITH?

A. Antoine ☐

B. Daniel ☐

C. Bailey ☐

2. DOES LOTTIE SMELL LIKE CAT
FOOD?

A. Yes ☐

B. No ☐

C. No idea, never sniffed her! ☐

I'm going crazy – this is a diary! No one else is actually
reading it so why am I trying to get imaginary people to
fill out a survey?!

Although if this somehow ends up in a random person's
hands . . . and if you ticked **1C** and **2A** then I'm sorry but
we can't be friends!!

8.45 p.m.

I hear a knock at my door and it's my mum coming
in with fresh laundry for me to put away. (She's like a
machine – we've only been back a few hours!)

'Look what I found in your denim shorts, Lottie,' she says, taking something out of her pocket.

I look up – it's the necklace Daniel gave me! I take it and turn it round in my fingers, suddenly feeling a rush of emotions.

'Everything OK, love?'

How do mums always seem to know when something is up?! It's proper spooky if you ask me.

'Yeh, I guess.'

'You sure?'

'I . . . I'm just feeling a bit . . . confused, I suppose.'

She comes in and sits on my bed. 'Let me guess – about boys?'

I couldn't help but blush. It's always a bit weird talking to your mum about boy stuff.

'Yeh . . . Antoine wrote me a letter saying he wanted to be my boyfriend . . . I really like him, but then I also really like Daniel too.'

'Look, can I be honest, Lottie?'

I don't know why she said that as it was clear she was about to be honest, whether I liked it or not.

'I don't mean to sound patronizing, as I know you hate that, but you are still so young. There will be plenty of time for boys, believe me. For now, you could . . . just hang out with people you enjoy hanging out with and not worry about the romance side of things quite so much?'

I smiled. 'That sounds like a good idea.'

She gave me a big hug. 'Thanks for telling me though. You know you can always talk to me about anything – right?'

'I know.'

I might complain about my mum quite a bit (OK, OK, more than a bit), but sometimes she can also be pretty cool.*

*Pretty cool for a mum anyway.

9.01 p.m.

WhatsApp from Jess:

> **JESS:** Hey! I forgot to say this earlier, but you know you said you sorted stuff out with Amber?

> **ME:** Yeh.

> **JESS:** Well, I bumped into her and Molly in town last week. We ended up going to Starbucks and it was really strange because Amber was being . . . really nice!

> **ME:** ☺ I guess being the school mean girl can be pretty exhausting.

> **JESS:** True. Do you think she's actually changed?

ME: Maybe. I hope so anyway.

JESS: Well, I was thinking, and you can say no obviously, as I know things have been difficult between you two – but should I invite her and Molly to come along to my birthday tomorrow?

I sighed and started chewing on my fingernail. It was a really tough one because it was tricky to figure out if Amber was being genuine this time.

I messaged Jess back . . .

ME: Yeh I think that would be nice. Xx

Deep down I knew it was time that I put this stupid feud with Amber to bed.

(9.15 p.m.)

Another message just popped up on my WhatsApp – it was from Daniel and I felt a weird mix of happy and sad to see his name.

DANIEL: Welcome home! Did you have a nice holiday?

ME: Yeh, it was great thanks! 😊

DANIEL: Cool! Be good to see you. Wanna go to the pier tomorrow?

ME: Sorry, I can't. I'm seeing my friends tomorrow. But I'll message you later in the week? x

DANIEL: Deal! x

I felt kind of bad leaving it quite open like that, but he didn't seem to mind. I just need a bit more time to figure things out in my head.

MONDAY 22 AUGUST
(JESS'S TWELFTH BIRTHDAY!)

What a day! The sky was blue and the sun was shining. I put on a pair of shorts and noticed that my legs had a tan – a very, very slight tan due to the factor-50 sun cream that Mum kept insisting I apply fifteen times a day – but a tan nonetheless.

I walked over to Jess's, holding her present, and rang the doorbell. She squealed when she saw me, and immediately tore open the wrapping paper, the biggest grin appearing on her face as she saw what was inside.

I'd got her custom socks with both our faces printed on them. I knew she'd be delighted because she's weird like that, and that's why we are BFFs!

'What else did you get?' I asked.

'I got football boots, hot-chocolate bombs, a sloth Oodie, MORE books – oh, and this,' she said, holding up a Polaroid camera she had hung round her neck. 'I'm going to take loads of photos to document today, so no nose-picking, OK?'

'I'll try my best,' I said, laughing.

We had a plan to meet Poppy, Molly and Amber at the bus stop to travel into town together. I was obviously a bit nervous about seeing Amber again, but I was determined that we'd try our best to get along because today was all about celebrating Jess.

I needn't have worried though. When we arrived, Molly gave me a big hug and told me how much she'd missed me, and Amber smiled and said, 'Hey, Lottie – wow, you look tanned! Did you have a good holiday?'

'It was great, thanks,' I replied and smiled back.

When we got to the Palace Pier, Jess handed out some wristbands that her mum had bought us that gave us unlimited rides for the day – it was SO brilliant! We went on the dodgems, the waltzer, the Crazy Mouse, the Horror Hotel and the Wild River – it was the first time I was tall enough to go on the Turbo Coaster too, which was epic! And then, because it was all free, we decided to do them all again.

When we were getting on the waltzer for the second time, I told the guy running it that it was Jess's birthday, so he let us go on it three times in a row and played 'Happy Birthday' through the sound system. We all sang along at the top of our lungs. It was hilarious.

Afterwards we all felt really dizzy and sick, but Amber was looking particularly bad. I quickly linked my arm with hers and took her out of the crowd to the edge of the pier and it was very lucky that I did because about ten seconds later she was vomming off the side. Much to the annoyance of a passing paddleboarder.

I held her hair out of the way and rubbed her back while
the others went to buy a bottle of water for her from the
refreshments kiosk.

'Thanks, Lottie,' she said.

'Don't mention it,' I replied. 'I'm very experienced in this
area, remember?'

She laughed. 'I feel much better now.'

After that we decided that we'd had enough of the rides, so we wandered down to the beach.

'Does anyone fancy getting something to eat?' asked Jess. 'My mum gave me enough money for a chippy tea for everyone!'

We all nodded our heads enthusiastically and headed over to the chippy to order. The smell of hot fish and chips and vinegar made my tummy rumble and I suddenly realized how hungry I was.

Once we'd got our chips, we went and sat on the beach to soak up the final rays of sun before Roxanne came to pick us up.

'How are things with Theo?' I asked Molly. 'Did you get to the top of the Chipometer of Love, yet?'

'Nah, we broke up,' she said.

'Oh God, I'm so sorry. What happened?'

'Don't worry – I'm totally over it. He thought having a relationship was distracting him from his footballing career.'

'Sounds like Theo!' I nodded. 'You sure you are OK though?'

'Yeh, I'm fine. To be honest, the Arsenal chat was getting a bit dull. I think we'll be better off as friends.'

'I could have told you that!'

'True.' She smiled. 'How about you and Daniel?'

'Hmmm . . . I'm not sure really. I mean, I like him but . . . I don't know. Having a boyfriend can be hard work and maybe I'm not ready for that yet.'

'Hang on . . . when did you get so wise, Lottie Brooks?'

I laughed. It had been a long time since we'd had a proper chat and it felt good.

It was nearly 6 p.m. by the time we'd finished our chips, but the day still felt baking hot. I kind of wished we'd brought our swimming stuff so we could go and cool off in the sea, but we decided to make do with paddling instead.

'Today's been so much fun,' said Jess. 'I've loved hanging out all together again.'

'Me too,' I said. 'And, as weird as it sounds, I'm almost looking forward to going back to school now.'

'WHAT?! Am I hearing this right? YOU ARE LOOKING FORWARD TO GOING BACK TO SCHOOL?!' shouted Jess in mock outrage.

'Nah, I know what she means,' said Amber. 'I'm looking forward to it too – it'll be good seeing you guys every day.'

'Do you know what this means?' said Molly.

'What?' asked Poppy.

'We need a new WhatsApp group!'

Jess started clapping her hands. 'Great idea! What shall we call it?'

'Dur . . . what do you think?' said Amber.

In unison we all shouted . . .

TUESDAY 23 AUGUST

Oh flipping 'eck, I'm down to my last few pages again. How do I fill up these pages so fast?! It doesn't seem two minutes since I wrote the first entry.

If feels good to end on a high though, and I can't stop grinning to myself when I think about yesterday – which is slightly annoying because my face is a bit sunburnt and it feels ouchy when I smile. (Turns out that Mum was right about the factor–50 after all – annoying!!) It's funny because I spent so long looking forward to my pier date with Daniel, but I ended up doing it with my friends instead . . . and it was even better than I'd imagined.

So now I guess it's time for my words of wisdom, huh?

Dear Lottie,

There was a time back when the thought of ever having a boyfriend seemed almost impossible. And look at you now – you have the opposite problem: too many of them!

In these past few months, you've gone from someone who has never been out with a boy to having had three dates, and there are several things you have learnt along the way . . .

Some stuff that I've figured out about love . . .

★ Never agree to going out with someone if you have no idea who they are.

★ It is impossible to eat ice cream on a date without dribbling it down your chin.

★ Bowling can be VERY dangerous.

★ If you have annoying, irritating, LOUD siblings who have no off switch, KEEP THEM AWAY FROM YOUR LOVE INTERESTS!

★ Practising kissing with fruit is kind of helpful, but use a banana at your own peril!

* There may never be a perfect time for your first kiss, but you should always make sure you feel 100 per cent ready.

* Looks aren't everything and it's important to have things in common too . . . Although whether a mutual love of cheese is enough, I'm still not sure yet . . .

* I am sure about this though – don't let boyfriend or girlfriend dramas come between you and your mates. (It's really not worth it.)

* Being in love with someone else is not the key to everlasting happiness . . . but being in love with yourself is.

* FINALLY, the most important thing that I've figured out is that it's OK to not have it all figured out yet – you are only twelve years old after all!!

Love Lottie
xxx

PS Oh, I nearly forgot – Jess gave me a few of her Polaroids from yesterday so I thought I'd tape some in for you here.

Aren't they just brilliant?

I mean, maybe I shouldn't say this, because I really don't want to jinx it, but I can't wait for Year Eight! I have a feeling that with these girls by my side it's going to be . . .

THE BEST YEAR EVER!

FRIES BEFORE GUYS

BEST DAY EVER

#FIVE FEISTY FEMINISTS

#THE QUEENS OF 8 GREEN

FRIENDSHIP TROUBLES,
MEGA CRUSHES, TERRIBLE
NICKNAMES AND NEW SCHOOLS.

WELCOME TO THE EXTREMELY
EMBARRASSING WORLD OF
LOTTIE BROOKS!

OUT NOW!

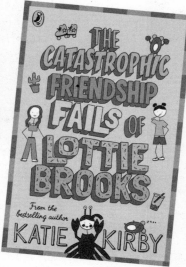

KATIE KIRBY is a writer and illustrator who lives by the sea in Hove with her husband, two sons and dog Sasha.

She has a degree in advertising and marketing, and after spending several years working in London media agencies, which basically involved hanging out in fancy restaurants and pretending to know what she was talking about, she had some children and decided to start a blog called 'Hurrah for Gin' about the gross injustice of it all.

Many people said her sense of humour was silly and immature, so she is now having a bash at writing children's fiction.

Katie likes gin, rabbits, overthinking things, the smell of launderettes and Monster Munch. She does not like losing at board games or writing about herself in the third person.